Favorite MISTAKE

LISA SUZANNE

FAVORITE MISTAKE
VEGAS ACES: THE WIDE RECEIVER
BOOK FIVE
© 2022 Lisa Suzanne

All rights reserved. In accordance with the US Copyright Act of 1976, the scanning, uploading, and sharing of any part of this book without the permission of the publisher or author constitute unlawful piracy and theft of the author's intellectual property. No part of this book may be reproduced or transmitted in any form or by any means, electronic or mechanical, including photocopying, recording, or by any information storage and retrieval system without the written permission of the author, except where permitted by law and except for excerpts used in reviews. If you would like to use any words from this book other than for review purposes, prior written permission must be obtained from the publisher.

Published in the United States of America by Books by LS, LLC.

ISBN: 9798352792773

This book is a work of fiction. Any similarities to real people, living or dead, is purely coincidental. All characters and events in this work are figments of the author's imagination.

BOOKS BY LISA SUZANNE

VEGAS ACES
Home Game (Book One)
Long Game (Book Two)
Fair Game (Book Three)
Waiting Game (Book Four)
End Game (Book Five)

VEGAS ACES: THE QUARTERBACK
Traded (Book One)
Tackled (Book Two)
Timeout (Book Three)
Turnover (Book Four)
Touchdown (Book Five)

VEGAS ACES: THE TIGHT END
Tight Spot (Book One)
Tight Hold (Book Two)
Tight Fit (Book Three)
Tight Laced (Book Four)
Tight End (Book Five)

A LITTLE LIKE DESTINY SERIES
A Little Like Destiny (Book One)
Only Ever You (Book Two)
Clean Break (Book Three)

Visit Lisa on Amazon for more titles

DEDICATION

For my three favorite people.

CHAPTER 1

Tessa

"Yes." I slap a hand over my mouth as the truth comes out of it, as if I could push it back in and reverse time and undo all of this so I could be the one to tell him first.

I didn't get to tell him first.

I was too scared. It was easier living in ignorance. I didn't know how he'd react, so I tempted fate, tempted Savannah, and that girl from the sex club, tempted all of this to come out before I did what I knew deep down was the right thing.

"See?" Savannah says snidely to Tristan. "You thought I was being a bitch, but I was always doing what was in your best interest. I was always thinking of you."

Tristan ignores her words as his eyes stay focused on me.

"I…I wanted to tell you," I stammer. "I tried to, but I—"

"Stop," he hisses, his nostrils flaring in anger. His neck and face are flushed, and his forehead shines with a soft sheen of sweat. I don't know if I've ever seen him look so angry before. "You had every opportunity to tell me before she did." His eyes harden as he glares at the women in front of him…none of which have done right by him.

He runs his hand through his hair as he tries to figure out his next move.

"Fuck," he says softly, and then a little louder, he yells, "Fuck!"

He moves to stride past me, but I grab onto his arm.

"Don't leave," I beg, tears coursing down my cheeks as baby girl kicks into my ribs. "Ah," I grunt. He yanks his arm out of my grasp, and I let go of him as my hand moves to my side.

"Are you okay?" my mom asks, and Tristan doesn't stick around to find out. "Honey, sit down," she says.

"I'm fine," I grunt out, and I don't sit. Instead, I rush out of the chapel as I try to catch him, but I'm over thirty weeks pregnant and he's an NFL wide receiver who was chosen for the Pro Bowl two years running thanks to his speed and agility. Even if I wasn't pregnant, he'd outrun me.

I don't even see him once I'm past the threshold of the chapel.

He's gone, and I don't know where he went. I look around desperately as I try to find him, but he's gone.

I suck in a deep breath as I try not to panic.

I'll find him.

I'll fix this.

I don't know how…but I will.

I can't go back in the chapel. I can't face our few guests who are still standing in there. But I don't have a choice.

Everyone's quiet, unsure what to do. After a few beats, Travis rushes past me out of the chapel, and then Luke follows him. Ellie stays. Tristan's parents stay.

And I turn around to face the people left behind.

"I have a grandchild?" Sue's voice breaks the silence first.

"Yes, Mrs. Higgins," Savannah says, handing her the envelope and papers that she's already taken out. "You do. And this one kept everything from all of you." She jerks a thumb in my direction.

Sue's eyes move toward my mother's. "You knew about this? You never told us?"

Savannah's eyes light with each bomb that goes off in this tiny room that suddenly feels way too small as she surveys the destruction she's causing. It isn't just Tristan and me. It's my relationship with his parents. It's my mom's relationship with her neighbors.

It's our entire life as it comes crumbling down around us.

"Yes," my mom says quietly, and I realize that my father is gone now, so even if we tell the truth, it'll only look like we're blaming somebody who isn't here to defend himself. "It's a long, complicated story, but the truth of it is that her father found the positive test and forced her to leave town."

Sue lets out a snorting sound, and Russell is quiet beside her, and all I can think is that Savannah ruined my fucking life and I want to fucking kill her.

I stalk toward her. "Are you happy now?" I hiss.

She stands a little taller as she tips her chin up. "I wanted you two apart, but I never wanted to hurt him."

I cackle menacingly. "Us apart *will* hurt him, you bitch!" I move to take a swing at her, but I'm too slow and she steps back.

"Hey, don't hit the messenger," she says, holding her hands up.

My eyes fall to the folder in Sue's hands.

Savannah said she had the birth certificate, the adoption certificate…does that mean our boy's information is in there?

His name? His parents? Where he lives?

Exactly how much did Savannah find out? What is in that envelope?

And…how? The records were sealed. If I…*the birth mother*…wanted that information, I wouldn't have been allowed it.

But she has it.

I turn toward Tiffany. "What the hell are you doing here? How do you have a part in any of this?"

"I knew you'd need someone to hold your hand after Tristan broke up with you. I'm here as your friend, Tessa," she says, and there's something in her eyes that I can't quite make out. Sarcasm, maybe.

"Bullshit," I say, and I move in behind her as a sudden realization dawns on me.

Dark hair about my length.

Same size as me, too—when I'm not pregnant, anyway.

I yank her hair, and she tries to tug out of my grasp as she yelps in pain, but I just grasp her hair more tightly in my fist as I look at the tattoo on her neck.

Angel wings that look to be in the shape of a heart with a date in the center. March twenty-first.

Not May twenty-seventh, as Walt first suggested.

"So it's *you*," I hiss.

I don't know what March twenty-first means to her…but then it hits me.

I left about a week before that.

She tattooed the date she seduced Tristan onto her skin.

"I don't know what you're talking about," she says, and she finally shoves her way out of my hold, smoothing down her hair.

My first thought is that I need to get in touch with Walt.

But the destruction is already done.

Whatever she's doing and how it relates to Savannah is meaningless. JustFans is meaningless. The sex club girl and the club…all meaningless.

Because nothing in my life has meaning if Tristan isn't in it, and he just walked out of it.

I could choose to dwell on that, to lie down without a fight, or I could do the opposite.

I've already been ripped away from him once. I will not allow it to happen again.

CHAPTER 2

Tristan

I run.

I'm sure I look like a fucking maniac as I literally haul ass through the hotel and out to the Strip in a tuxedo, but I had to get out of that goddamn room before I suffocated in it. My legs carried me all the way outside, and I know I'm leaving behind problems that I can't outrun, but I just need a minute.

Or a day.

I handed my phone to my mom when we were taking pictures, and she probably still has it in her possession. It's for the best, though. There's nobody I want to talk to right now.

Instead, I want to live in the knowledge I own now for a minute before I'm expected to respond to any of it.

I have a kid.

A child walks this Earth who is one-half me and one-half the only girl I ever loved.

The only girl who ever had the power to break me.

She broke me once before. It's happening again, but this time…I'm the one who's walking away. It's the only way I can feel any semblance of control over anything right now.

All I ever wanted was to have a big family with Tessa.

I don't care how or why she gave up that child. The fact remains that I confessed everything to her—the shameful secrets I never wanted anybody to know—as we vowed that we'd be honest moving forward.

And the whole time, she kept her secret under wraps. My secrets had nothing to do with her, though. Her secrets had everything to do with me.

How different would my life be if I would've had a child at eighteen? Would I be a professional football player right now? Or would I be sitting behind a desk, miserable with my life as I work to live and support my family instead of having the type of career most people could only ever dream about?

I'll never know the answer to that question because the right to it was stripped from me.

I have a lot of other questions, too, but none of the answers matter more than one.

Is my kid happy being raised by someone else? Savannah might have the answer to that—or at the very least, she might be able to give me the names of the parents so I could get in touch and find out for myself.

If he's happy, I can't just walk in and interrupt his life. Not after he's lived seven years with somebody else.

But what if he isn't?

He's mine. He should be with me.

I don't even know his name.

For seven years, a boy I helped create has walked this planet...and I had no idea.

My chest cracks with the knowledge. My stomach heaves. I feel like I might be sick as heat pools behind my eyes.

I don't know where to turn. I don't know what to do.

I hate Savannah for ruining our day, but I hate Tessa for keeping it from me.

I also have no idea what she has been through. I have no idea what torture she's endured...but it couldn't have been that bad if she could look into my eyes and keep something so important from me while she kissed me, fucked me, promised to marry me.

I stop when I get to the street, and I stare out over the traffic. Cars move along, some weaving in and out to try to get to the next light first, horns honk, people move. Life continues as usual as if my ex-wife didn't just deliver life-altering news to me, as if my world didn't just stop turning.

I don't know where to go. I don't know where to turn. A cab pulls to a stop at the red light in front of me, and his light is on—meaning he's taking passengers. I open the door and slide into the back.

"Where to?" he asks.

I can't go home…I don't have a home here anymore. I was going to stay with Luke and Ellie while I figured that one out.

I can't stay here, where I'll be forced to face the liars and manipulators inside.

Only one place comes to mind.

"The Vegas Aces practice facility," I say.

Twenty minutes carry me away from the lies and toward the only place that feels like home. I stare quietly out the window the entire time, focusing on the landscape, the cars, the people, the mountains, the palm trees…anything but what I just found out.

The Complex is pretty much empty when the cab driver lets me out. I don't have my keycard, so I can't just walk in, but I spot Coach's car in the lot, so I figure he must be around here somewhere. I can't text him to come let me in since I don't have my phone, so I perch on the cinderblock half-wall out front and wait for someone to come by.

I loosen my tie, take off the tuxedo jacket, and roll up my sleeves. My watch tells me it's eighty-one out right now, but it feels like about a hundred ten as the sun starts to lower in the sky.

I'm only out there maybe fifteen minutes when the door opens and Coach spots me sitting there. He's clearly done for the day and on his way toward his car to go home, but he stops.

"Higgins?" he asks, his brows drawing together as he takes in my appearance.

"Hey, Coach. I, uh…don't have my credentials."

"Come in," he says, and he walks in with me.

We pause in the lobby, and I lean against the wall for a beat.

"You don't need to hang around. I just needed some place to go, and nowhere felt like home quite like this place." I knock on the wall beside me. Even I can recognize the sullenness in my own tone.

"What's going on, kid?" he asks. "What are you doing here…and why are you dressed like that?"

"Runaway groom," I mutter, and then I can't help a small laugh. I must look ridiculous right now.

Coach looks at me like I'm a little crazy, and I slide down the wall until I'm sitting on the floor.

"I was supposed to be getting married about a half hour ago. And then my crazy ex-wife showed up with papers claiming my would-be wife birthed my child seven years ago. She never told me, but she admitted it was true. So I fled, and this was the first place I thought to come."

"Whoa," Coach murmurs. "That's quite a day."

"Tell me about it," I huff.

"Want some good news?" he asks.

I nod as I glance up at him.

"The brass upstairs issued your extension today. I've got the paperwork with your new contract in my email," he says.

I press my lips together. This should be the greatest day of my life.

Instead, I can't seem to muster up any enthusiasm at his words.

"That's great," I say, my voice flat.

Coach slides to the floor beside me. "This too shall pass." He says the words quietly, and when I don't respond, he continues. "That's what my dad used to tell me whenever I hit a rough patch. *This too shall pass.* He wasn't wrong, but it never helped me feel better in the moment, you know? You have every right to feel how you feel, but I'm going to tell you what I tell every player when something gets them down, and this applies both on the field and off. Focus on the next play, kid. You hear me? Focus on the next play."

I nod as I blink, trying to grasp onto what he's saying.

If I let this pull me under, I'm putting a whole lot at risk.

"I guess I just have so many unanswered questions that I'm not even sure what the next play is," I admit.

"Who can answer those questions?" he asks.

I lift a shoulder. I'm not sure if anyone can, and the person who was supposedly the reason behind all of this in the first place is six feet deep in the cemetery back in Fallon Ridge. My fists itch, though, and what I wouldn't give to slam one in that motherfucker's face.

I hate him with an unreasonable amount of force. I hate her right now, too, and I really hate Savannah even though a tiny part of me is grateful I found out about all this before I made Tessa my wife.

Is that why she was rushing into this wedding? She gave some bullshit reason about my dad being there while he's physically able to be, but did she really just want to jump into it before her secret came out, before Savannah told me the truth?

These are questions I need answers to, but I'm too fucking worked up to go back there right now.

"Thanks, Coach," I say. "You've given me a lot to think about."

"Why don't you come home with me for the night?" he suggests. "Mama Mo can whip up a casserole and you can take a night in a neutral zone with somebody who has your best interest at heart." He pats his chest.

"I don't want you and your wife going to any trouble for me."

"Trust me, kid, Monique *loves* when I bring home boys from the team," he says, referring to his wife who's basically the mom of the Aces. "Since we never had kids of our own, she feels like you're all her boys."

I look over at him gratefully. "What kind of casserole?"

He chuckles, and then he helps me to my feet. He waits while I change out of this tux into some clothes and shoes I find in the locker room, and we head out to his car.

CHAPTER 3

Tessa

I finally collapse in the back row of the chapel. I need a drink but I'm still fucking pregnant.

"The JustFans thing," I say to Tiffany. "It was you all along."

Her eyes dart nervously to the sex club girl whose name still escapes me.

"And you," I say, my eyes moving over to her. "The girl from the club whose name I can't remember. How do you calculate into all this?"

"Brandi," she says, holding a hand to her chest like I care. She grins. "That was my idea." The way she says it makes it seem like she's proud of that fact.

My brows dip. "*Your* idea? It was *your idea* for someone to impersonate me online on some porn site?" I struggle as I stand to yell my next word. "Why?"

"A porn site?" my mom echoes, standing beside me.

"It's a long story," Brandi says, ignoring my mom. "But as it turns out, Savannah hooked us up and Tiff is a good friend of mine now."

"You're…you're…" I sputter.

"Besties," Brandi fills in. "Savannah and I met ages ago here in Vegas, probably even before Tristan and I met. But these two met at your little fair thingie and we just—"

"Joined forces," Savannah finishes. "It was my idea, actually, for the three of us to work together to break you up. I tried to get Christine Foster on board, too, but she blocked my number. And then I happened upon that *very* interesting information about you giving up a baby all those years ago." She flips her hair over her shoulder, and she's so damn *smug* standing in the middle of the aisle, *my* aisle, that rage fills me.

Before I can make a move toward her, though, Sue steps out into the aisle, and she lifts her hand and slaps Savannah across the face.

The loud sound echoes in the room, and Russ makes a move to stand behind his wife in a show of support.

"Shame on you," she says to her former daughter-in-law. "I never liked you, but you've proven today just what a horrible choice my son made when he married you in the first place. And you," she says, spinning around to turn toward Brandi, "dressed like a streetwalker in this nice chapel…my son would never even give you the time of day. And I don't know what you think you're doing," she says, turning to Tiffany, "but your obsession with my son and Tessa is totally out of hand. It has to stop."

She walks down the aisle past the offending women and stops in front of me. My heart pounds in my chest as I fear what her words to me are going to be.

And then her eyes soften as she takes my hands in hers. "I can't imagine what you've been through, Tessa. I can't say I'm not devastated by what we've learned today, and it breaks my heart that you've kept this from us as long as you have. But I know you, and I know your mother." She snags her bottom lip between her teeth just like her son does as she tries to hold it together. "I wish things came to light in a different way, but it doesn't matter that you didn't marry him today. You are family, and we will work through this together."

She wraps her arms around me, and I sag against her in relief.

"Thank you," I sob.

Russell hugs me next. "Life is short, kiddo. We fix our mistakes…even when they weren't ours to make."

I know he's right.

I'm just not sure how, exactly, I'm supposed to fix this one.

Travis and Luke walk back into the chapel, both out of breath.

"Couldn't find him," Travis says, and he slides into the back row of the groom's side. He pulls his phone out of his pocket while Luke joins Ellie. "I'll try texting again."

"I have his phone," Sue says quietly. "He handed it to me before pictures, so wherever he is…he's without his phone."

"Shit," Travis mutters.

"Any ideas where he might've gone?" my mom asks.

"His room?" I suggest.

Travis shakes his head. "Tried that."

"We checked the bars around the hotel and out front, too," Luke says.

"I have an idea of where he might be," Brandi says, and I glare at her.

She's wrong.

He would *not* go to a sex club on the day his wedding was ruined.

"Shut up," I say to her. She's not supposed to talk about the club, anyway, and I'm certain he wouldn't want his parents knowing about it.

Travis shakes his head at Brandi, and I glance over at him. His eyes meet mine, and that's when I know. He's a member, too, and some mutual understanding seems to pass between us where he knows I know about it.

What other things happen underground with celebrities that the general public has absolutely no knowledge of?

"Maybe he went up to our room," I suggest, but it's a stupid thought. He ran out of the chapel to get away from me. He wouldn't run straight upstairs to the one place where we could be alone. Baby girl kicks me in the ribs again, and I gasp. The dress suddenly feels too tight, and I feel like I just want to go lay down. It's been a taxing day, and I'm supposed to be taking it easy.

None of this is taking it easy.

"I need some air," I say, and I dart out of the chapel. I head up the elevator to our suite just to check, and when I finally get to the room, it's empty.

I chug an entire bottle of water, and then I sit alone in a chair in the bedroom where we were supposed to spend our night making love to one another as a profound sadness over everything I've lost washes over me.

CHAPTER 4

Tristan

Monique Thompson makes a damn fine casserole, but the homecooked meal isn't enough to even make a dent in the constant dull ache spearing my chest.

I'm alone with my thoughts in the Thompsons' guest room, and I never should've called it an early night. I don't even have my damn phone to scroll in here.

I realize it's only been a few hours, but I can't help wondering whether this will ever get easier.

It feels like I'll be cursed to a life of pain, and I'm not exactly sure what I did to deserve it.

I guess I had premarital sex, and that was enough for Bill Taylor to cast his judgment and determine the punishment for our sins.

I think bitterly of the old man again as I wish he were here so I could speak my mind to him.

I'm sure my mother is worried about where I am, but I don't really have the inclination to get in touch just yet. I'm fine, and we always lived by the *no news is good news* motto anyway.

Besides, it's not like I'm not aware that I can't outrun my problems. I will eventually have to go back and face everybody, but I needed a minute—or a night—to myself to work through what I just learned.

How can I ever trust her again? Do I *want* to trust her again?

These are the thoughts that plague me. I'm not sure what the answer is yet. It's too fresh.

I'll get in touch with my parents tomorrow, but I have this strange feeling the hurt from today is just the tip of the iceberg. It won't get better tomorrow, or the next day, or the next. It'll get much, much worse as the shock of it all wears off and I have to learn to live with the reality before I start to feel any relief.

And then what do I do? Find my kid?

My parents are here through Sunday, and at some point I should see them, maybe tell them goodbye. Get my phone back.

It's not their fault any of this happened, and none of it changes what my father is going through. I still want to spend as much time with him as I can, but I can't go back to Iowa.

I never should have.

I'd learned to live with the pain of losing her the first time. I'd learned how to manage it over the years apart. Time doesn't heal all wounds, as the saying goes, but the pain isn't as sharp after a while.

And now all the progress I made has been ripped open and torn to shreds. This is even worse than the first time. The first time, she was just gone. I was young, and eventually I figured heartbreak was just some rite of passage.

This time, I didn't just lose the girl. I lost fucking *everything*. I was planning my life around someone who couldn't be honest with me.

I blow out a breath.

I need to talk to her. I need to know why she lied. I shouldn't have run, but I did.

And now, I'll run back.

I need answers.

I head out to Coach's family room, where I find him and his wife watching television. "Can you call me a ride back to the Strip?"

"You sure, kid?" Coach asks.

I nod. "Thank you for feeding me dinner and for making me feel like I have somewhere to turn. But I can't run away from this."

He gives me a sad smile. "You're a good kid, Tristan. I'm proud of you for coming to that decision all on your own."

He reaches into his pocket without getting up and taps around a minute. "Woods is on his way. Should be here in about fifteen minutes."

My chest tightens. He was there. He witnessed the fallout.

And he's my best friend here in Vegas.

Somehow Coach knew that. He knew instinctively that Travis was the right person to call.

And that's somehow a major comfort in this unclear time. I'm in the right place. Vegas is home now.

"Thanks, Coach."

He nods, and fifteen minutes later, Travis rings Coach's bell. He hands me my phone with a look of concern, but I don't have the energy to look at it right now. I slide it into my pocket.

He and Coach chat a second, and then I give both Coach and Mo hugs before Travis and I leave, clutching my tuxedo in my arms as I stare out the window on the way back.

"You okay, man?" he asks.

I shrug. "Not really."

"You want to go back to the hotel or you want to chill at my place tonight?" he asks.

"I don't want to face her, but I know I have to." My voice is quiet.

"How are you handling all this?" he asks, turning out of Coach's neighborhood.

I blow out a breath. "Not well. Is it any wonder I have trust issues when it comes to women? I've surrounded myself with manipulators and liars."

"But it doesn't change how you feel about Tessa," he says.

"No, it doesn't. I will always love her. But I think this is one of those instances where the old cliché about whether love is enough comes into play. I'll be honest…I don't know if it is. I don't know if I can get past all this," I muse as I stare out the windshield. "And what about the kid? Do I even want to know? What if he's happy? I can't just walk in and interrupt his life. But what if he isn't? What if I could take him out of a bad situation?"

He doesn't have to give me the old speech about how he's here to listen and how I have to answer these questions for myself. Instead, he helps me figure out the answers on my own—eventually. And that's what makes him such a valuable friend.

"What do you want to do?" he asks carefully.

"I don't know," I murmur.

"Can I tell you something I've never told anybody before?"

I glance over at him, my brows drawn together as I wonder what confession he's about to make.

"I'm a father."

"You're…" I trail off.

He nods. "I have a kid, a ten-year-old girl. I've never met her, so I guess I'm not so much a father as a sperm donor."

"What?" I'm frankly shocked by his revelation.

"It's complicated. I slept with one of my mom's friends before I headed off to college. She and her husband couldn't have kids, and she was a lonely housewife, hot as fuck, and I was a horny teenager. When I came home for winter break, she was over for my parents' annual Christmas party. I was sneaking beer from the cooler on the patio and nobody else was out there but the two of us. She told me she was pregnant, and she said it was mine, but nobody could ever find out. I was eighteen and had my entire future in front of me, so even though it felt wrong, I agreed. She and her husband are giving that girl a good life, I guess."

"Wow," I say, scrubbing a hand along my jaw. "You've never met her?"

He shakes his head. "I didn't go back home much after that. You know how it is." He keeps his eyes on the road. "I was busy with football, and I thought it was smarter for everybody involved to just let it go."

"And now?"

He shrugs. "I'm a twenty-eight-year-old man who doesn't visit home ever so I don't have to run into her and my kid."

"Do you want to meet her?"

"I think about her all the time," he admits softly. "But she's not mine to have. She was never meant to be mine."

I think about that. Did the child Tessa and I share have a similar fate? He was never meant to be ours?

For the briefest glimmer of a second, I can't help but wonder what Tessa's been going through all these years. We shared the same hopes and dreams for our future together, and we would've made it work even if we had a kid when we were young.

It's easy to say that now. It would've been much harder to actually live it.

"If I would've stayed and fought, it would've changed everything for everyone," he says. "She and her husband might've divorced, and I wouldn't have had the means to raise a child back then. I had a one-fucking-percent chance of making it to where I am now. And she—she had virtually no skills aside from spending her husband's money. That kid has a better life because of the sacrifices I made."

His tone has just the smallest bit of reticence in it.

"You sure about that?" I ask.

"It's what I have to believe. If I allow my mind to go any other way..." he trails off, but he doesn't have to finish.

I guess I get it more than I ever thought I could, although I'm not sure how to process what he just told me.

He pulls his car to the front of the Venetian.

"You ready?" he asks.

I shake my head. "Nope."

He chuckles. "Go get your girl...or go do whatever you have to. My door's open anytime. Come stay with me if you'd like."

"Thanks, man. And thanks for telling me about your girl."

He presses his lips together and nods once, and then I get out of the car and head inside.

CHAPTER 5

Tessa

I'm crying—still—as I stare out the window at the lights blinking down below. My mom and Tristan's parents just left, and I'm all alone.

I'm not sure I've ever *felt* the loneliness as much as I do in this moment. I felt alone when I had the baby, and I felt alone when Cameron told me to *take care of it*. But nothing could ever have prepared me to lose Tristan again. Nothing could have ever prepared me for this moment right here as I prepare to go to sleep on the night of what was supposed to be my wedding day.

Everyone said all the words and tried to keep me calm for the baby's sake, but nobody really knew what to do. And since none of us knew where he went and nobody could get in touch with him, I'm not just feeling lonely.

I'm feeling worried. Anxious. Scared.

I told Brandi he wouldn't go to the sex club, but what if he did? What if that was his default, the place where he could unwind and just be himself after learning the things he learned? What if he finds some girl to have sex with there?

What if I don't know him at all?

I know it's ridiculous to even think that way. I know him. Of course I do. I know him better than anybody, and that's why I know he won't run forever. Eventually he'll come talk to me.

Just as I have that thought, I hear a knock at the door.

I said *eventually*. There's no way it's him.

Still, I practically run toward the door just in case, and when I peek through the peephole, a sense of calm washes over me.

He's changed from his tuxedo into athletic shorts, an Aces tee, and sneakers, and he's just as hot in these clothes as he looked in that tux.

I toss the door open, and I rush into him, tossing my arms around his neck. I hold tightly onto him, but I never feel the familiar slide of his arms around my waist.

He just stands there clutching his tux, and a dark chill freezes my veins.

I slowly pull back as all my hopes and dreams that he came back for me are crushed in one simple rejection. "Come on in," I say, opening the door wider to allow him to enter.

Anxiety claws at me as I try to keep a calm exterior, and I walk back to the chair I just vacated to answer the door. He sets his tux on a table before he sits in the chair beside me, and I let him lead the conversation.

"I have a lot of questions," he begins, "but now that the initial shock has worn off, there's one I keep circling back to. Why didn't you tell me?"

I clear my throat and keep my gaze out the window. "What would've changed if I had?"

He doesn't respond.

"I wanted to tell you, but I was scared. We talked so much about how the future means more than the past, and I guess I just thought I was sparing you the pain of knowing."

He shakes his head as he leans forward, elbows on his knees and eyes out the window. "Don't act like some martyr who was only protecting me. That's bullshit and we both know it."

I suck in a breath. "I admit I took the easy way out, but I was going to tell you once the baby came. You told me not to get stressed, to keep the baby safe, and keeping the past tucked away seemed like the right move." I set my hand over my stomach.

"Another bullshit excuse."

"Why'd you come here if your only plan was to tell me I'm spouting bullshit? I'm telling you my truth, Tristan. I know you don't like it, and I don't blame you…but I haven't exactly had the easy end of this, either. Living with what happened has been enough to drive me to really dark corners over the last seven years, and I didn't really see the light again until you stepped back into my life." My voice is soft as I make the confession.

"Then start at the beginning," he says.

"My dad found the positive test, and without warning, without *anything*, against my will and my mother's, he shoved me into the back of a car that took me to my aunt's house in Chicago. He was ashamed of me not just for having premarital sex, but for being so stupid as to get pregnant. His words, not mine. His only goal in life was to *look* like the perfect pastor of his congregation, and so he sent me away. He made up some story and my mom and I didn't have a choice but to stick to it. He'd made sure I had no way of getting in touch with you. With home." I can't help the sob that escapes me, and my voice trembles with my next sentence. "I had the baby, and I never even got to hold him."

Tears run down my cheeks, and he gasps softly at my admission.

"The nurses took him from my body and never let me look at him. My parents signed away my rights. I was young and scared, and I didn't even know I *had* rights. I didn't know that at seventeen, it was up to me whether I wanted to give him away or not. My dad made sure I didn't know any of that. And as far as I knew, the records were sealed. I tried to get a copy of them once, but I wasn't able to."

I glance over at him, and he's still refusing to look at me.

"Today I learned that since the adoption was through a private agency, they still had records of the original birth mother. I don't know how Savannah got them, but she did. I tried looking you up after I had the baby. Once he was signed over to the new parents, I was allowed to go to school in-person, and then I could access the internet. But by that time you were in the middle of your freshman year football season. You were a starting player, and I knew that was rare for a freshman. I saw photos of you, and you looked like you'd moved on. I didn't know what would've changed if I was able to track you down and tell you, so I just…I held onto the heartbreak myself. I didn't want to put you through the hell I'd been through. I didn't want you to have to feel all the horrible things I was feeling."

He's quiet a beat. "It was an act. All of it." He closes his eyes and rubs his forehead with his fingertips before returning his elbows to his knees, his eyes still out the window. "The last seven fucking years have been an act. Football is the only thing that kept me going. I may not have known about the baby, but I sure as fuck felt the same heartbreak you did."

"I'm sorry," I whisper. I don't know what else to say. "Please tell me we can work through this."

He continues to stare straight ahead. "I don't know if we can." He finally tears his gaze from the window to look at me. "How do I ever trust you again?"

"I don't know," I admit. "But their goal was to break us. We can't let them win."

He huffs out a mirthless chuckle. "They did win, Tessa. I'm broken, and I don't know if this is something I'll ever come back from." He stands. "I just need some time. I wanted to come here to get some questions answered, and I guess I did." He starts walking toward the door.

"So where do we go from here?" I ask, scrambling to stand as quickly as someone seven months pregnant can with the giant belly and the aching back.

"I don't know." He sighs, and his eyes flick down to my stomach. I can't help but wonder whether he'll still want to be a part of her life…if his words that she's his are still true. If he'll stand by that or if he's leaving her because he's leaving me—which tells me she was always only mine, and he was just accepting her into his life because she was a part of my package.

God, this is all so complicated.

"I'm going to stay here in Vegas a while," he says. He opens the door. "I've got OTAs coming up in a few weeks anyway." He steps through the doorway, and it feels very final. My heart aches with his next words. "You go back to Fallon Ridge. Take care of yourself and the baby. I'll see you around."

He turns to walk down the hallway, and the door latches shut behind him.

A hollow echo sounds down the hallway, and I feel it in my chest—hollow now, too, because he just walked away with my heart in his hands.

CHAPTER 6

Tristan

I head up to my parents' room. I booked them a suite, and I assume they're still in it.

I still haven't looked at my phone. I just don't have the energy.

I knock on the door, and my dad answers. He immediately grabs me into a hug, and his wordless greeting as he holds me seems to be exactly what I need to finally let it out.

The heat that has pressed behind my eyes all day and has given me a monster of a headache finally hits the boiling point as it tips over the edge of my lids.

I'm not an overly emotional guy, but the last event that triggered tears was the first time I lost Tessa…so I suppose it's appropriate that they come back on a day like today.

My mom comes in to hug me from the other side, and I hear her sniffle. She's crying, too, and I can't think of anybody in the world who could hold me up in a time like this better than my parents can. They were there for me the first time I lost her. They'll be there for me again now, however I decide to handle the events of today.

"I was so worried about you," my mom finally says, pulling back.

I move out of my dad's embrace then sniff and wipe my face as I fight for composure. "I'm okay. I'm here." I give her a quick hug, and then we all move over toward the sitting area. My parents each take a chair, and I lay across the couch.

"Where did you go?" my dad asks.

"I was suffocating in that chapel with all the drama, so I went to the only place that felt like home—the Complex," I say, staring up at the ceiling. "I ran into Coach and he took me to his house, fed me dinner, and then he called Travis to come get me."

"Have you spoken with Tessa?" my mom asks.

I nod. "Just came from there."

"How'd you leave it?" she presses.

"I told her I don't know where we go from here, but I'm staying here in Vegas a while so I can figure it out." I clear my throat. "I want you two to stay here, too. I'll pay for the doctors and surgeries out here, Dad. I need to be with you…but I just can't go back there."

"I understand," my dad says. "And I don't blame you, kiddo. But Vegas is your home. Iowa is ours." He says it gently to soften the blow.

I chew my bottom lip for a beat. "You'll keep me updated, right?"

"Of course we will," my mom assures me.

"I can come back for next week's surgery," I offer. "Maybe stay in Davenport."

My dad shakes his head. "You stay here. There's nothing you can do back home anyway."

We're all quiet a beat, and then I remember what Coach told me. "Coach Thompson said the brass approved my extension."

My mom yelps, and my dad's eyes widen as he sits forward in his chair.

It's been a hard day, and this gives us a good reason to celebrate.

"He did?" my dad asks, wonder in his voice.

I nod, but I don't move from my position laying across the couch.

"I think this calls for a drink, son," he says, and he glances at my mom, who nods. "Let's all go downstairs a while."

"I don't feel much like celebrating," I admit.

My dad stands and towers over me—an unusual occurrence given that he's five inches shorter than me. "We've had a string of shit news lately, and we finally have a reason to celebrate. Now get your ass up and come have a drink with your parents."

I can't help a laugh as he grabs my arm and yanks me up, and then the three of us head downstairs for drinks and slot machines.

Later, I fall asleep on the couch in their hotel room.

My parents have seen all the sights in Vegas, so on Saturday we hit their favorite spots, and I stay at the hotel with them one more night. When Sunday morning arrives, it's time to say goodbye. I walk them down to the lobby, and we find Tessa standing there with her mom.

I don't look at her. I can't.

I'll fold if I do, and maybe that's the right thing to do. Maybe I should just give into the pull I've always felt toward her. Maybe we really do belong together.

But the cut is still fresh, and I still don't know how to deal with the lies. I'm not sure I'll ever have an answer to that, but I need some time away to think it through…because if I don't take the time away, I'll never give myself the space to really figure out what I need. I can't think rationally when I'm around her because the connection between us just constantly pulls me back into her orbit.

I guess I need to find out who I am and what I'm made of before I commit to a life with her.

I should have done that anyway. I got so excited about the possibility of forever with her that as soon as my divorce was final, I jumped right into things with Tessa.

I haven't given myself the space to heal those wounds yet, either.

And so I'll take a little time away to rediscover who I am…to do right by myself.

I say goodbye to the four people in the lobby, saving Tessa for last.

"I don't want to leave," she whimpers as I give her a hug. I do my best to keep it friendly, but she clings to me, and I don't want to let her go. "I'm so scared."

"I know," I whisper back. "I am, too." And then I forcibly pull back from her.

The car pulls up just then, and my parents and Janet all rush to get their luggage toward the back so the driver can heave it in.

It gives Tessa and me a minute alone.

"It isn't goodbye forever, right?" she asks.

"I don't know," I admit.

She grabs my hand and squeezes it, and then I wave to the group of them as I walk away.

I can't watch as they duck into the back of the car.

I can't watch as it pulls away.

I can't watch as Tessa leaves with a piece of me. I guess I won't know whether I need that piece or not until I experience this fresh new life without it.

CHAPTER 7

Tessa

I stare out the tiny airplane window pretty much the entire way home. My mom sits quietly in the seat beside me, and I'm not sure if she's quiet because she doesn't know what to say or because she's giving me space.

It feels very much like I'm grieving a loss. I manage to keep the tears at bay, but taking off from this place and leaving it behind me feels wrong. I'm supposed to be moving here. I'm supposed to be married. Instead, I'm going home alone and it feels like I'm leaving a piece of my soul here…because I am.

Tristan is my heart and soul and walking away from him is hard. I'm giving him the space he needs to find it in his heart to forgive me. I know we both want this and want to figure out how to make it work, but he's struggling with how to trust me after I kept something so huge from him.

I don't blame him, and I think back a few days to when I found out about his tryst with Tiffany and his time on the third floor at his club. I was hurt by those secrets that didn't have any effect on me. The difference is that the thing I kept from him wasn't like that. It has a direct effect on him. It involves him.

I hate that I'm the one who caused this pain. I want to blame Savannah, or Tiffany, or even Brandi, but the truth is I'm the one who kept a secret that had the power to break us.

I was planning on telling him at some point, but it's out now. My intentions no longer matter.

I can't stop seeing the hurt in his eyes when I asked him if this is goodbye forever. I have so many questions about the future. I didn't even think to ask if I go home to our house on the corner now or if I should move back in with my mom. Is it his house or ours? He said he bought it for me, and I want to be there, to feel him there and see him in every corner…but it might be too painful to be there without him not knowing the answer to any of these questions.

The baby kicks as we touch down in Chicago, and I can't help but feel the loss more strongly as this is the place where I was forced to give up the baby that is half me and half Tristan. The same place where I got pregnant with the baby I'm carrying now, the place I left so Cam could keep his little secret and I could have this baby.

This place represents so much loss, and yet if I look hard enough, I can still find hope.

He's out there.

The child Tristan and I share…he's somewhere out there.

Savannah somehow manipulated her way into getting all the information in her hands, and Tristan's mom has it now. All I have to do is ask.

But do I want to know?

Of course I do. It's something I think about every single day of my life. Is he okay? Is he happy? Is he healthy? Those are the only things that matter, and Sue has the papers that could lead me to the answers.

He's been with the only parents he's ever known for seven years. I can't just walk in and claim him as mine even if I wanted to.

But what if he isn't happy? What if he isn't well-adjusted? What if he hates his situation?

Is that something I could change?

Is it even within my rights to?

I have no idea how any of this works. How Savannah got the information is completely beyond me, but whatever she did…it couldn't have been legal. Not when I was the actual birth mother and I was turned away a few years ago.

I ride in the backseat with my mom while Russ drives us back to Fallon Ridge and I contemplate what the next step should be. The car is awkwardly quiet on the way home, and I'm sure Russ and Sue have about a million questions, but I'm thankful they're not asking them right now.

When we pull onto Main Street a little under three hours later, we drive past the house on the corner. Everyone in the car turns to look at it.

That's our house, and I have the urge to go there.

But I also don't want to be alone.

Luckily, I don't really have to make that decision. After we say goodbye to Tristan's parents, I walk with my mom toward her house.

"Stay with me a while," she says. "I don't want you to be alone with the complications you were having before."

I press my lips together and nod. "Thanks, Mom. I appreciate it."

We unpack and settle in, and she makes me dinner, and we're both quietly lost in our own thoughts for most of the evening. She heads to bed at her usual time, and I head toward my bedroom window.

I sit on the windowsill and cry.

At nine fifty-seven, I text Tristan.

Me: Back in FR. Sitting by the window wishing you were here.

It was a simpler time despite its many complications.

He writes back after a few minutes.

Tristan: Thanks for letting me know.

That's it. That's all he says.

He could bare his heart, or I could tell him what's in mine, and instead, all I get is just a simple thank you for letting him know I made it home safely.

I search for some way—any way—to extend the conversation.

Me: Are you okay?

Tristan: I don't really know.

His answer is honest, at least, and as I search for what to say next, another text comes through from him.

Tristan: I can't do this. It's too hard right now.

My chest cracks and what pieces were left of my heart seem to break all over again.

He's staying in Vegas.

It's too hard for him to even text with me.

What about the baby?

I want to ask, but I'm too afraid.

He made promises to me, to us, and I want to know if he still wants to be a father to the baby I'm carrying now. He fell in love with her as he held my hand at every appointment, as he rushed me to the ER, as we watched her on the screen at my ultrasound appointments. It's not her fault that I screwed up, and I hate that she might be punished for my actions.

I hate that maybe he's not just leaving me, but leaving us.

I hate my father for forcing me to do the unthinkable.

I hate the destruction this one secret has caused.

I hate Savannah for exposing it before I was ready to.

But beneath those layers of hate, my love for Tristan burns strong along with my love for the baby I'm carrying…and in this time of darkness, it's that light that will keep me fighting.

CHAPTER 8

Tristan

Three weeks after the day I was supposed to marry Tessa and instead had my entire world blown apart, I'm not any closer to figuring out what my next step should be.

Instead, I've thrown myself into workouts and preparing for the upcoming season.

The news broke that the Aces signed me to a fifth year about a week after our failed attempt at a wedding, and I had to put on a happy face for the media. And truthfully, I *am* happy to be signed to the Aces. I'm ecstatic. I have my amended contract in hand with the guarantee of a fuck of a lot more money. It's everything I've ever wanted…except there's one big piece missing.

One piece I almost had within my reach. One piece I can't quite seem to get over.

My dad's surgery went well, a bright spot in an otherwise drab landscape, and while I wanted to go home to be with him during his recovery, both he and my mother assured me he was fine. We've talked every day, but otherwise, I've been focused on football.

The Aces OTAs—Organized Team Activities--started yesterday with a three-day focus on workouts. I've had nearly three full weeks of intense workouts on my own, so I'm in better shape than most of my colleagues.

We're all hurting, but I'm hurting less than they are after their off-seasons filled with too much beer, too many carbs, and way too many women.

Women just cause complications.

And that's why I've avoided them altogether. I'm not partying. I'm not drinking. I'm not going to nightclubs or sex clubs or bars.

Instead, I'm staying in Travis's guest room, though I'm not much of a houseguest. He participates in workouts with me some days, we play video games together, and then he goes to the club while I stay at his place playing more video games or calling it an early night so I can run before the sun comes up and the Vegas heat starts to kick in.

We just finished today's organized workouts, and tonight is Troy Bodine's big charity event.

He told me to bring a date.

I'm going solo.

The only person I'd even consider going with is very pregnant and hundreds of miles away. Oh, and there's that whole secret wedged in between the two of us that I still can't quite wrap my brain around.

I asked my mom if she had the papers.

She confirmed she does.

She asked me if I wanted the information.

Not yet, I'd told her.

I want it, but I'm terrified of it. I want it, but I don't know what to do once I have it.

I won't risk his happiness, but I want to know his name.

It's not a name I gave him, or a name Tessa gave him. It's the name someone else decided they'd call him for the rest of his life.

I've tried over the last three weeks to put myself in Tessa's shoes.

Absolutely she got the short end of the stick. Absolutely she suffered.

But she had no right to keep it from me.

I get why she kept it buried with the past for seven years. We weren't in touch, so that part of it isn't what gets to me. It sucks, but it's in the past.

What gets to me is the fact that she had every opportunity to tell me once we reconnected, but she didn't. She didn't bother.

And *that* is what hurts.

I blow out a breath and glance at myself in the mirror as I try to push those feelings aside. Tonight is supposed to be fun. I'm not sure how it will be since *nothing* has felt *fun* lately, but I'll give it a try.

Travis decided to go solo, too—maybe in solidarity with me, but I think it has more to do with the fact that he's been brooding about something he doesn't care to talk about. Or maybe I'm not being a good friend. Maybe I haven't been the most approachable guy lately for him to feel like he has someone to talk to in his corner.

I'm not sure I have the capacity to change any of that right now, though. I feel like any advice I dole out might be along the lines of *don't trust women*. That's probably not what he needs to hear right now.

I'm wearing a suit tonight, and the last time I dressed up was the day I was supposed to get married. It was the day my life changed forever, as if my life is split into two periods now. Clueless Tristan before I knew, and heartbroken Tristan after. Maybe it's even more than those two. Before Tessa left and after. Before Tessa broke me for the second time and after.

My phone buzzes with a text.

Savannah: *Can we please talk?*

It's the hundredth time she has sent the exact same text message.

I told her no at first.

Then I started ignoring her.

I scroll to her contact, my finger hovering over the *block* button when something strange hits me.

It's like divine intervention as some voice tells me not to do it, and I realize why. If I block her, I might never learn the truth.

And I need to know how she got her hands on the adoption files.

According to Tessa, those records were sealed. The only way someone who *isn't* a parent to that child would be able to get those records is through criminal means, and my lovely ex-wife is still on probation.

Instead of responding, I call my lawyer.

I'm supposed to be meeting Travis in the kitchen to pregame before we grab a car to tonight's event, but I need to make this call.

I glance at the clock. The office is closed—of course, given that it's a Saturday night after hours—so I leave a message. "Richard, hi, it's Tristan Higgins. I have some questions regarding my ex-wife's probation and what would happen if she broke another law. I don't have evidence, but I think it may be worth looking into. Give me a call back when you can."

And then I text Savannah back. I'm not sure what comes over me, but suddenly I just have the need to fucking *do* something.

I guess this is it.

Me: *I'm on my way to Troy Bodine's charity event tonight. Meet me there.*

Savannah: *I heard about it, but I don't have an invitation.*

Me: *Then you'll be my date.*
Savannah: *[thumbs up emoji] See you in an hour in the lobby.*

It doesn't surprise me she's willing to drop whatever she's doing to meet me. She's desperate to get in touch, desperate to hang on to me, desperate to keep living the life she's been living plus my fat new paycheck as the cherry on top, and all that desperation has made her fucking delusional if she honestly believes I'm inviting her to be my date to this thing tonight with no ulterior motives.

I meet Travis in the kitchen, and he's midway through a tumbler of whiskey.

"You spending a little extra time primping tonight, Princess?" he asks.

"Fuck you," I say. "No. I was securing a date."

He laughs, but I don't. His smile falls quickly as his brows knit together. "Who?"

I offer a menacing grin. "My ex-wife."

"Savannah?" he says, his eyes bulging.

I nod as I grab the bottle of whiskey and fill a cup to the top. Fuck etiquette. If I'm going to take my ex-wife on a date, I'm going to need a whole lot of alcohol dulling the senses.

"Why?"

I chug down a few sips. "She's been asking to talk to me, and I told her we can talk at the charity event tonight. I was seconds away from blocking her when I thought of that old saying about keeping your friends close."

"Enemies closer?" he correctly guesses.

I nod. "I'm done with her bullshit. Believe me. But if I can get her close, I might be able to find out how she got that information in the first place. It couldn't have been through legal means, and if I have evidence she broke the law, I can bring it to my lawyer. And then the next step is getting her ass thrown in prison, where she belongs."

"Or you could just, you know, take her out to the middle of the desert, or Thelma and Louise her," he suggests.

"Thelma and Louise her?" My brows furrow in confusion.

"You know that old movie where they drive off a cliff at the end." He takes a sip of his drink.

"Uh, thanks for the spoiler alert, man. I hate her, but I still wouldn't wish death on her." I chug down more of my drink.

He laughs. "Then you're a stronger man than I."

"A taste of her own medicine wouldn't be the worst thing to happen to her," I admit. "I just have to play it the right way."

We finish our drinks just as our ride shows up, and we head toward the hotel where Troy is holding his event. I don't see Savannah, for which I'm grateful as an entire line of photographers snaps photos upon our arrival.

Troy greets us with Sapphire on his arm in the main lobby, and they seem happy together. I can't help but remember when Troy punished Sapphire and withheld both her orgasm and aftercare. I wonder if I'll always think of that moment when I see them together. I remember feeling strange about it, like he was being cruel to her—but the way she's smiling tells me whatever happened between the two of them all those months ago was consensual. Mutual. Welcome, even.

I spot Victor Bancroft greeting guests in the doorway of the banquet hall even though this is Troy's event. Maybe they're closer than I realized, which makes sense given the fact that they own a club together.

I peek into the banquet hall and see about a million cameras in there, too. Clearly he wants this event highly publicized, and I'm starting to think it was a terrible idea to invite Savannah here.

"Where are your dates?" Victor asks.

"Didn't bring one," Travis answers a little sullenly.

"Mine is meeting me here in a bit," I say.

He gives Travis a look I can't quite decode, and I get the feeling he was hoping we'd bring along dates that match our social status so he could invite them to preview the club.

I like Victor, but I get the feeling his main objective in life is making money.

Shit, he'll *really* like my date, then, since they share the same goal.

I should warn him not to invite her to Coax, but before I get the chance to say anything, he says, "You haven't been to the club recently. Why not?"

I lift a shoulder. "I've spent the off-season out of town."

"You're here now, though," he points out.

"Right, for OTAs. We're expected to be at workouts, and I'm usually pretty beat by the end of the day," I say. It sounds an awful lot like an excuse, particularly given the fact that my teammates are probably still showing up, but I don't really care. It's my truth.

"You'll come by after tonight's event, yes?" he asks.

I shake my head. "No, sir. I think I'd like to cancel my membership."

He gasps, clearly surprised, as if once you're in you'd never even so much as dream of getting out.

"I'm certain Jade can change your mind," he says, and he flicks a finger in the air. Less than three seconds later, a woman sidles up beside me, her tits pushing into my arm. "Meet Jade."

"Nice to meet you," I say, feeling very uncomfortable. It appears Victor is the one running the show over on this side. I'm trying to believe it's because he's gravitating to us as members of his club. I look around and see lots of other celebrities here who *aren't* members of Coax, and it's only then I realize I know very little about this charity event.

Is it actual charity? Or are Troy and Victor just raising money and expanding membership for the club?

Hard to tell.

"And you," she says.

"Travis, I have a girl for you as well." He flicks another finger. "Meet Raven."

Her tits are up against his arm, too, and I can't quite tell what we're supposed to do with all this. Are they members of Coax? It's been a while since I've been there.

A flashbulb goes off in my face, and I realize I'll be splashed on the tabloids with Jade on my arm tomorrow.

"I'm so sorry, Jade, but I do have a date meeting me here shortly. If you'll excuse me." I beeline toward the bar, ditching Travis who already seems preoccupied with Raven… *and* Jade, whose tits are now pressed to his other arm.

Whatever he was being quiet about earlier…he seems okay now.

I head out to the lobby to wait for Savannah, not totally sure I'm doing the right thing here. But we're in public and at a charity event. I hardly think she'll make a scene at such a high-profile event.

She walks in, and it's funny how I used to think she was so beautiful…because now all I can see is the ugliness that resides within. Lies, manipulation, and causing pain are the things that keep her going.

Her eyes seem to shift from the coolness of entering a room full of unknown people into warmth as she spots me. She strides across the room, her gait obviously showing her level of confidence, and she stops just in front of me.

"Looking handsome as always, Mr. Higgins," she says.

"Thanks," I murmur, refusing to return the compliment even though on the surface, she does look gorgeous. I force myself to draw her into a quick embrace, kissing her cheek as I do in an attempt to show civility in public. "What did you want to talk about?"

"Already down to business. Can't we have some fun first?" I force a chuckle. "Of course."

We head into the banquet room, and I introduce her to Victor simply as my date rather than giving her the complicated titles she deserves. My ex-wife. The bane of my existence. The master manipulator who ruins lives.

What the fuck am I doing?

I walk over to the bar with her, and she orders a glass of wine while I grab a refill. I spot several retired baseball players I've seen at the club before, and they're all talking to Cooper Noah, the retired player I met at Ben Olson's Big D Bash.

"Let's dance," she suggests, and I offer her my elbow as I escort her to the dance floor. The slow tempo of the song forces me to take her in my arms, and I can't quite act good enough. I'm thankful I'm holding a drink in one hand and she is, too, because I'm having a hard time being this close to her. I'm not drunk enough for this.

And that sparks an idea. She always had looser lips after a few glasses of wine, and so I set out to get her drunk. I chug my whiskey and set the glass down on a table nearby, and the buzz is just starting to cloud over me. She finishes her first glass, too, and I walk her back toward the bar for another before we return to the dance floor.

"We had some good times together, didn't we?" I ask once we're dancing to a more up-tempo song and I'm no longer forced to hold her close.

She offers a small smile. "A lot of good times. Don't downplay what we shared."

"You're right. I'm sorry."

She's sipping her wine too slowly.

"What did you want to talk to me about?" I finally ask again.

She clears her throat. "I just wanted to reiterate that I really was looking out for you, Tris. I always wanted our relationship to be mutually beneficial. It wasn't just about me marrying into the league again so I could get locker room access. That was a byproduct of falling in love with you, and I promised you before we were married that I would make you a household name. I promised I would always fight for you. And I promised I would give you the truth no matter how hard it was to hear."

I nod. She did promise me those things, but I never imagined in a million years that she would take it so far as to investigate people from my past.

But for as horrible as she is, she's also incredibly savvy. She must've known somewhere, somehow, that Tessa was always in my heart even though I never so much as spoke her name to Savannah. And that gut feeling of hers was enough for her to take a deep dive into Tessa's history.

The way she held onto it until it was convenient for her is a different story. The fact is that she told me she'd give me the truth, and when it was a good time for her, she did.

I wish she hadn't done it on my wedding day to Tessa, but I'm still glad I know.

I tell her that.

"Thank you for telling me," I say softly.

Damn, that whiskey's working quick.

"Someone had to," she says, her tone matching mine. She tips her chin up. She's in heels, which puts her a little closer to my height, but she still has to stand on tiptoes to brush her lips across mine.

I jerk back out of her grasp.

Fuck no.

Not for all the goddamn whiskey in the world.

CHAPTER 9

Tessa

"What the hell?" I murmur.

It's late, and I haven't heard from Tristan since I sent that text to him the day I got home. I've thought of him every single day, and I've typed out hundreds of text messages only to delete them.

Ellie called me a few times to check up on me, and she told me that this will all blow over. She was so confident, in fact, that she started training me via Zoom on how to work in public relations. She's sent me videos to watch and has me studying both Instagram and TikTok along with different aspects of life in the league.

I've learned a lot, that's for sure.

And it's as I'm studying charity events in Las Vegas that I come across a news item from tonight.

It's a photo of Tristan…and his lips are on Savannah's cheek.

Savannah.

The woman who interrupted our wedding, detonated a bomb, and broke us both.

His lips. Her cheek.

I search and search to find more, but I can't find a thing. Mostly it's photos of who is at the event, and it's like a Who's

Who of the celebrity scene in Vegas. I wonder how many of the celebrities in attendance are members of Tristan's special little club.

I wonder if he's been back since everything went down.

I wonder if he goes there to blow off steam.

I wonder if he can still say he's never had sex with anybody at the club.

I force the thought away.

It appears Tristan walked in with Travis, but at some point, Savannah showed up. I can't confirm that anywhere, though, and instead, I keep going back to the photo where his lips are on her cheek.

His lips. Her cheek.

Is he back with her? Did they clear the air? Is he grateful she told him the truth when I didn't?

My stomach lurches, and I feel like I'm going to be sick. I stand to rush over to the bathroom, but I can't seem to move quickly enough through the thick black spots clouding my vision.

Did I stand up too fast?

I'm not sure, but I'm suddenly falling, falling, falling.

And then darkness.

"Tessa!"

"Tessa, honey! Wake up!"

My eyes fly open and I wake with a loud gasp as I try to heave in air.

"Honey, are you okay? You're white as a sheet and I think you must have fainted!"

"I...wha—what?" I can't seem to form a thought yet. I sit up slowly with my mom's help, and she hands me the glass of water from my nightstand.

"A loud bang woke me up, and you know I sleep through everything. I ran in here to find you passed out on the floor."

"I fainted?"

"Let's get you checked out," she says. "Come on, honey." She helps me stand, but I'm definitely wobbly on my feet. She sits me on the bed, and she runs to my closet. She pulls out some flip flops and slides them on my feet, and then she leaves the room for a second and comes back with her own sandals on, her purse slung over her shoulder, and car keys in her hand.

"I'm fine, Mom. Really," I say.

"I'm not taking any chances after that bleeding scare a few weeks ago. Come on, we're going to the ER."

I blow out a breath, knowing fighting her on this is futile. It's ten at night, and we should all be sleeping.

By the time we get to the hospital, I feel fine except for the constant twisting in my gut and the pressure in my chest as I think about that picture.

I don't mention it to my mother.

As we're waiting, she taps away on her phone.

I keep mine put away.

I can't stop thinking of that image, and even though I feel okay now, I can't stop worrying about the baby.

I can't stop wondering if he's at that event in Las Vegas right now with his ex-wife.

If I'm the last thing on his mind as I sit here in an emergency room waiting for a doctor to tell me whether everything's okay with the baby.

It's over two hours later before we get any news at all from the doctor. "Everything looks fine," he says. "Fainting in the third trimester is actually more common than you'd think. All those hormones changes can cause low blood pressure, so I'd recommend taking some preventative measures. Get out of bed slowly, or even out of a chair or off the couch. Don't skip meals, drink plenty of fluids, and take short walks to help with circulation, but don't stand too long. Any questions?"

I shake my head. "Thank you, doctor," I say.

He nods and leaves, and then I'm discharged.

My mom drives us home, and she chatters the entire way. I tune her out as she talks about taking care of myself and how glad she is we went in just to confirm everything's okay and how she texted Tristan to let him know I was in the emergency room…

"Wait. What?" I ask, suddenly on high alert.

"When we were waiting for the doctor, I texted Tristan," she says.

"What? Why?"

"Because he should know what's going on. I know he's not talking to you right now, that he's *figuring things out* or whatever he said, but he said he wanted to raise this baby with you. That means he should be informed when I have to take you to the ER in the middle of the night because you fainted."

"You didn't *have* to take me," I mutter, but it doesn't matter. They're the only words I can think to say, and I don't even hear her next words over the loud roar in my head.

"I'm glad I did. And I'm glad I texted him, too."

She makes no mention of whether he wrote her back.

But he hasn't texted me, either, to check on how I'm doing.

And with that thought, my chest tightens a little more along with the knot in my stomach as that image of his lips on her cheek floats back into my mind.

CHAPTER 10

Tristan

"What is going on here?" a voice behind us demands.

I'm definitely drunk now, but I'm still focused on my objective, which is to get Savannah drunk and then get her to spill how she got her hands on the adoption paperwork.

I think. That *was* the plan, right? Whiskey is clouding my intentions, and I'm really not sure anymore.

Travis has been by to check on me a few times, but he knows my plan so mostly he's leaving me alone.

But that voice…

I spin around to face Brandi.

Fucking fuck.

I'm already playing nice with one psycho from my past. Now I have to do this with another one?

What fresh hell is this?

What sort of monster was I in a previous life to have to endure this punishment in this one?

"Are we all friends again?" she asks, circling her finger in the air between my ex-wife and me.

No. That's a big, flashing, fuck hell to the no. "We're getting there," I say instead, circling my arm around Savannah's waist and drawing her into my side.

Brandi laughs. "Can I join in on the fun? I've always wanted a threesome with a married couple."

"Of course you can," Savannah slurs, and she's probably at the exact right point where I can start to snag information out of her but now Brandi is here, ruining the moment.

I give Brandi a look that clearly says not to mention Coax in front of Savannah, but she seems a little drunk herself, so I'm not sure the message gets through. And I'm not sure Savannah doesn't already know about it anyway.

"Did you just get here?" I ask, and she nods.

"I had a performance tonight, but Victor invited me to come by after," she says.

"Oh?" Savannah asks. "How do you know Victor?"

Brandi winks at me. "We're old friends." Thankfully she leaves it at that, so she must've gotten the meaning of my secret look.

But knowing Savannah, it won't be long until she knows about the club and the fact that I'm a member…if she doesn't already know. Then somehow she'll figure out a way to snag a membership for herself, and it just feels like no place is sacred anymore. I just want to get the hell away from her, but she keeps turning up.

"You're missing your third," I say dryly.

Brandi laughs. "Tiff's back in Iowa. She took down the JustFans and decided to lay low awhile so your girl doesn't press stalking charges." She rolls her eyes. "That Tiffany girl is *not* subtle, I'll give you that."

"Why'd she agree to do it?" I ask.

"She wants Tessa's life. But, then, don't we all? The perfect, dreamy man, the happy ending." She smiles a little wickedly. "But not so happy for her now, am I right?"

I feel a little sick at the way she's talking about Tessa, so I grab another drink to get away from them for a minute.

We dance as a threesome for a bit, and then I excuse myself to the restroom—mostly because I need a breather from these two women. It's hard keeping up the act even with the amount of whiskey I've had tonight.

"You doing okay, man?" Travis asks, grabbing my arm on the way to the restroom. He's still with Jade, the girl Victor reserved for me earlier, and I'm not sure where the other one went…nor can I recall her name.

"I'm okay," I say, glancing at the woman by his side. "Just heading to the john."

"Let me know when you're ready to get out of here." He makes eyes at me that tell me he doesn't want to spend the night with Jade, and I nod.

"Soon. Just need a few more minutes with my ex-wife," I say.

He nods, and I head to the restroom. I slide my phone out of my pocket on the way and see I have a new text from Janet.

My brows dip as I glance at the clock. The text came in a couple hours ago, but even then it had to be after eleven in Iowa.

My heart leaps up into my throat.

Janet: *Just wanted to let you know Tessa is in the ER. She fainted earlier but seems to be doing fine now.*

"What the fuck?" I murmur as fear races down my spine. She fainted? Is she okay? Is the baby okay?

It's nearing midnight here, which means it's getting close to two in the morning there. But she never wrote back to tell me Tessa's fine, or they're on their way home, or anything. Just that she's in the ER and our baby might be in danger and oh my God what the fuck am I doing here in Las Vegas while she's in Iowa suffering without me?

My immediate reaction is that I need to get the fuck out of here and on a plane so I can be by her side. It's not a rational thought, particularly given the fact that there are no flights out until morning and I'm too drunk to drive anyway, but protecting my girl and our baby is my first instinct.

My girl.

And our baby.

I dial Janet, but it goes to voicemail.

I dial Tessa next, and I'm shocked when she answers. "Hey."

"Are you okay?" I ask.

"I'm fine. We're on our way home," she says.

"Oh, thank God. Your mom's text scared the shit out of me," I say. "The baby's okay?"

"Yes. I guess I just stood up too fast and low blood pressure can be common in the third trimester. We're fine. Heading home to get some rest." She sounds exhausted, and I'm sure she is after a stint in the ER.

"Okay. I'll check in on you tomorrow." *I love you.* I feel like I should say it. I *want* to say it.

I do. I love her so goddamn much that it hurts, and it's that love that has broken me twice now.

Am I such a masochist that I'd subject myself to the possibility a third time?

Or is the third time the charm?

I'm not sure, but I do know I need to carry out the plan I started tonight.

Maybe if I can take care of one problem, I'll have a clearer head to tackle the next.

CHAPTER 11

Tristan

I have a pounding headache when I wake up for the final day of OTAs the next morning.

I have regrets.

Many of them.

It was stupid to drink the way I did last night. Stupid to try to get information out of Savannah. Stupid, stupid, stupid.

But…at least I woke up alone this morning. Could've been worse, I guess.

I force myself to make it through workouts, but I have to run out of the weight room midway through my first morning session to puke up half a gallon of whiskey.

I'm dehydrated, but Adrian is there with electrolytes to help me get back on track. Travis laughs at me, along with Jaxon, and I don't know what Cory did last night but he looks even worse off than me. He and Jaxon weren't at Victor's charity event, but if everyone was there, nobody would've been at the club, so I assume that's where they went.

I wasn't able to get anything out of Savannah, but I planted the seed. Maybe it wasn't as stupid as I thought when I first rolled out of bed.

The day feels incredibly long, but as it winds to a close, the wide receivers meet with Coach Jeff in a classroom then make plans to head to the restaurant across the street to grab a bite for dinner. Everyone's here, and all six rostered wide receivers from last year came back to play for the Aces again.

It's like seeing family as we sit down at the barbecue joint across the street like we did once a week last season, and I realize how much I've missed these guys while I've been away in Iowa.

It's so strange to feel like half my world is here and half of it is somewhere else.

I'm suddenly starving after staying away from food the majority of the day. By this point, I've sweat out any remaining whiskey, and I'm feeling much better.

Travis sits beside me, and Cory's on my other side. Across the table from me is Josh, and on either side of him sit Cason and Damon.

We catch up, chatting about what we've been doing in the off-season, but I sit as a quiet listener today rather than contributing much to the conversation.

In fact, I don't say anything at all until Josh directly asks me. "What about you, Higs? What have you been up to?"

I lift a shoulder. "Divorced, engaged, interrupted wedding, pregnant girlfriend I broke up with after the ex-wife brought some information to light."

Everyone just sort of stares at me a minute, and then Josh lets out a nervous laugh. "Sounds like you're ready to get back on the field."

I blow out a breath. "It's been...interesting. I'm definitely ready to have the stability of the season back."

I say the words, but I'm not sure how true they are. I'm not sure about much of anything at this point.

If I'm on the field, I'm not with her. But I haven't been with her for the last three weeks, either.

I still don't know how to trust her, and I'm still not sure I'm ready to go back.

But I also don't want her to be alone as she navigates the last weeks of her pregnancy. I know she's not alone. She's got her mom, and my parents are right next door. My mom told me Tessa has been staying at Janet's, and a certain sadness fills me that the house on the corner is sitting empty.

It's my fault. I never told her to go there, or maybe she doesn't want to be alone.

It's a good thing she wasn't alone last night when she fainted.

"Higs? Higs!"

I hear Josh trying to get my attention, and I finally snap to it. "Sorry. What?"

"Are you okay, man?"

"I don't know," I admit, and I feel heat pressing behind my eyes.

Are you fucking serious right now?

I'm not about to fucking *cry* in front of my teammates, but I can't stop thinking about what could've happened if she *had* been alone last night.

If her mom hadn't been there.

Why the fuck I wasn't there.

Why I'm letting this thing from the past hover over me as I allow it to keep us apart instead of letting her talk to me about what happened.

Savannah is winning because I'm letting her win.

I can't let her win.

I press my palms to my eyes in some attempt to make it look like I'm just tired rather than about to cry. I draw in a deep breath through my nose and let it out slowly, and then I chug a little water. When I glance around, all five of my teammates are staring at me wordlessly.

"Yeah," I finally say. "I'm okay. I just have some mistakes I need to fix."

"We're here, man," Josh tells me.

"I know." I glance around, and nobody's really within hearing distance of our table. We're set in the back for privacy anyway, and the music's loud enough that if I lower my voice, this will stay between us.

And then I proceed to blurt out the entire story to my brothers.

"Long story short, I just learned my high school girlfriend left our senior year because she was pregnant. It turns out the baby was mine and her dad sent her away to have it and give it up. I never knew about it until Savannah interrupted my wedding to the same girl to tell me about that baby. And now...I don't know how to feel. It's like it's all coming full circle. She's pregnant, knocked up by another dude who wants nothing to do with it, and I vowed I'd raise that kid as mine. I proposed to her. I want to spend my life with her. She agreed to move out here, but how can I trust her when she could keep such a big thing from me?"

Travis sits silently beside me, already knowing the story—hell, being a *part* of the story since he was there—but the others stare at me as if I've grown two heads.

I expect them to tell me to run far, far away, to just find women willing to be in it for one night because it's easier than dealing with relationships...but they don't say that at all.

Instead, it's Josh who steps up first. Josh, who happens to be Ellie's brother and who also happens to be married to Ellie's best friend. Josh, who is a father now, a guy who is eight or nine years older than me, who I watched on television his rookie season and cheered for since he played for the Bears, the team I cheered for. Josh, a man who I respect and consider a mentor.

"Maybe I'm an eternal optimist, but I like to think everyone's just doing the best they can with what they have, you know? Do you know why she kept it from you?"

I shake my head. "Not really. She said something about how it wouldn't have changed anything, and how she was going to tell me after the baby was born. I kept telling her not to stress, not to worry about the past."

"So she was just doing what you told her to do?" he asks.

I shrug. "I guess."

Damon pipes in with a question next. "Has she ever done anything else to give you reason not to trust her?"

I think back over our time together, and while my immediate gut response is that I never knew her at all if she could keep this from me, I can't really think of another time when she broke my trust.

Josh's words replay in my head. *She was just doing what I told her to do.*

I told her not to tell me what happened when we were apart. That was on me because I wasn't ready to tell her about Tiffany or Coax.

Am I any better for keeping things from her?

Or am I setting a huge double standard where I expect her to tell me every detail about our past but it's okay for me not to share?

"No," I finally admit. "But she left me once, and it broke me."

"Because her dad made her," Travis says. "She admitted that much. Didn't she tell you she wanted to get in touch, but by the time she was able to, you'd moved on?"

I nod.

"Think about what she's been through, man," Josh says.

"I have," I protest, but while I've thought about it, I'm not sure I've ever really tried to place myself in her shoes. I suppose

I allow myself to cut out on those thoughts early rather than really living in the pain and heartbreak she must have endured—that she's *still* enduring.

She didn't just lose the baby. She also lost me, and none of it was what she wanted.

And then when she found herself pregnant again, Cameron Foster told her to take care of it.

Jesus Christ.

It's an epiphany a little too long in the making.

I can't change what we've done, but I can go forward with a more understanding heart. It's what we both deserve.

I don't have a lot of time to waste, but I do need to take care of a few things here before I head back to get my girl.

The first of which is my ex-wife.

CHAPTER 12

Tristan

Me: *How are you feeling?*

I keep my Monday morning text to Tessa casual, but I have to know how she's feeling after her rough weekend.

Her reply comes quickly.

Tessa: *Exhausted but otherwise fine. Thanks for checking. I miss you.*

I don't respond as I type out a message in a different conversation…this one to my mother.

Me: *I'm ready.*

I send the text, and less than a minute later, a bunch of photos come through.

She was waiting for me, and she came through.

But that's what moms are for, right?

My heart thunders in my chest as I look at the first image she sent.

Certificate of Birth.

My eyes go to the first line. Child's Name.

Handwritten in the small space is the name Logan James Wesley.

Father James Wesley.

Mother Miranda Wesley.

The birth certificate makes no mention of the biological parents.

I look at the next page, and it has James and Miranda Wesley's current address listed in Chicago, Illinois. It also lists their phone numbers and email addresses.

It makes sense since that's where Tessa was sent to have the baby. She lived there for almost seven years, and he was right under her nose.

I wonder if she has looked at these papers. I wonder if she's gotten in touch. I wonder if she has looked them up on Facebook like I'm tempted to do.

I can't see her doing that without me…and yet I'm sitting here wondering if I should.

My phone notifies me of a new text while I'm still staring at the contact information. There are more images my mother sent me, likely with the information about the adoption agency and who knows what else, but I click to answer the text when I see who it is.

Richard Redmond: *Is now a good time to talk?*
Me: *Yes.*

"Good morning, Richard," I answer when my phone rings ten seconds later.

"Tristan, hi. Got your message. What's going on?" he asks.

"My ex-wife interrupted my wedding with information that I have a child that I didn't know about," I begin. "He was given up for adoption, but she couldn't have gotten this information using legal means. The records were sealed. If I could prove she did something criminal to get her hands on them, what are we looking at?"

"I'd need more information, obviously, but considering the fact that she has moved and crossed state lines, both of which are issues while on probation, you've already got a case against her," he says. "Add even a misdemeanor to that, and she'll be looking at prison, especially given the EPA's issues with her last offense that landed her on probation in the first place."

"She isn't allowed to cross state lines?" I ask.

"Not unless she was granted approval. She could drive, obviously, and likely hide it versus flying, where there are records of everyone on board."

"She was in Iowa," I murmur. "I have plenty of people who could corroborate that."

"What's your angle here?"

"I want her to pay for her crimes." My voice sounds tired even to me, and it's because I'm so fucking done with her. I'm so fucking sick of her shit. "She has done nothing but make my life hell since I married her, and I'm just done with her getting away with the shit she pulls."

"Send me whatever evidence you have, and I'll get my team on it. She'll pay, Tristan. We'll make sure of it."

"Thanks, Richard," I say, and I cut the call.

I still need to find out how she got that information, and it's with that in mind that I send her a text.

Me: *Are you free for lunch today?*

She writes back almost immediately.

Savannah: *I'm always available for you, baby.*

Gross.

I think about where to meet her. I don't want to invite her to Travis's place, but I don't want to go anywhere public, either.

I guess public is safer. I pick a place close to where I'm at now.

Me: *O'Leary's at noon?*

Savannah: *I'll be there.*

I walk in a little before noon and grab a corner booth tucked away from the action—not that there's much action at a sports bar on a Monday before noon.

I'm halfway through my first beer when she walks in, and I call the server over immediately so I can start plying Savannah with alcohol as she slides into the booth across from me.

"You pick up drinking since the divorce?" she asks. She leans in a little. "Does it help ease the pain?"

I sigh. This is going to be a long fucking lunch.

Eye on the prize, Higgins. Keep focused.

The truth is I need it to dull her prickly edges, but I can't exactly admit that to her. "Nah, just on break so I'm having a little fun." I hold up my glass and chug the rest down, and when the server brings by Savannah's wine, I order another along with my standard chicken and veggies meal.

Savannah orders a salad with no dressing, and it makes me miss my cheeseburger and fry eater back in Iowa.

"So what have you been up to?" I ask.

"Oh, you know. A little of this, a little of that. I've started working with charities. My probation officer says it looks good." She lifts a shoulder.

"Where are you living?"

She laughs. "Like you care. Come on, Tris. What's this lunch really about?"

I blow out a long breath as I glance down at the table then up to meet her eyes. It's *Go Time*, Higgins. "I guess I just want to thank you." I'm lying through my teeth, and I hope she buys what I'm selling.

Her brows shoot up. "Thank me?" She sets a hand modestly on her chest. "For what?"

"For unapologetically telling the truth." I grab my phone out of my pocket and pretend to check a message. "Sorry, Travis has been texting me all morning." I act like I'm silencing it as I quickly open the voice recording app and hit record, and then I set my phone on the table face down.

She laughs—cackles, really—and then her eyes move to mine. "Oh, Tris." She pauses when she sees I'm not laughing. "Wait. You're serious?"

I nod. "I can see now that you were just doing what was best for me. You wanted me to know the truth about my past. You wanted me to know that I was with the wrong woman, and you were right. I never should have been with someone who could so easily lie and manipulate me." She has no idea that I'm actually talking about *her* with those words, not Tessa. But I'm letting her believe what she wants so I can get the truth out of her. "I just have to know something. It's been eating away at me. How the hell did you find all this out?"

She shrugs. "It was easy. I've known the stuff about Tessa awhile. People talk when they're offered money, and I started interviewing people in your town. Tiffany was one of the first, and when she told me your girlfriend had disappeared under mysterious circumstances, it became my mission to uncover those circumstances."

Tiffany Fucking Gable.

Of course it started with her. When she and Savannah were talking during the craft fair, they must've already known each other.

People talk when they're offered money. Is that considered bribery? I guess if she threatened to expose something it might be, but that's also blackmail…something she has plenty of experience with.

"I did it for you, baby. We didn't have the best marriage, but I want you back. I want to try again." She looks up at me from lowered lashes, and it's frankly disgusting.

She is disgusting.

But I have to play her game. "I want that, too. I want to be with someone I trust, and you've proven that I can trust you."

She looks surprised as her eyes meet mine. "You…you do? You want to get back together?"

"It'll take some work, but the charity event, and lunch today—they're leading us somewhere, you know?" I leave out the fact that they're leading us to the evidence I need to fucking bury her.

Maybe I should call up Victor Bancroft and let him know he should cast me alongside him in his next movie, because I'm giving an Oscar-worthy performance right now.

She nods.

"You just keep proving I can trust you, okay? That's what's going to make this work." I chug more beer, doing my best to fill my mouth so I don't say the wrong thing.

"There was a nurse at the hospital…she was newer, but she had all the hot goss for me."

"The hot goss?" I ask, my brows crinkling in confusion.

"Gossip," she says as if I'm stupid. "Anyway, this nurse *hates* her job. Totally regrets getting into nursing, so I told her I could give her some money if she spilled what she knew. It's all about finding out what motivates people, you know? I guess her aunt worked at the same hospital years and years ago, and she talked about how great it was, blah blah blah. Anyway she told her a story of this poor girl who had to give up her baby, and the trail led me to a private adoption agency. I turned on the charm and got the papers. Voila."

"You turned on the charm?" I ask, sickened by her story and her complete and utter lack of a conscience.

"Don't be mad, especially since we're working our way back to each other, but I figured out what motivated the guy at the agency. One rather lackluster blow job later and he suddenly had a whole lot to say." She shrugs, clearly not regretting what she did to obtain the papers my mom sent me this morning.

"He didn't have anything, but he directed me to the place that did, and that's where I took everything."

"Thanks for all you did to help me," I finally say.

Our food comes, but suddenly I'm not very hungry at all.

I don't know what to do with this information, but I pretend another text from Travis comes through, and I quickly end the voice recording, save it, and attach it in a text to Richard along with a brief message: Hope this is enough for you.

I hit the record button again, and I pray she'll say something else I can use so she'll finally get what's coming to her.

CHAPTER 13

Tessa

"Oh, Tris." A pause. "Wait. You're serious?"

My brows crinkle as I listen to the message Tristan just sent me along with the text that said, *Hope this is enough for you.*

Is that…Savannah?

I hear Tristan's voice next. "I can see now that you were just doing what was best for me. You wanted me to know the truth about my past. You wanted me to know that I was with the wrong woman, and you were right. I never should have been with someone who could so easily lie and manipulate me."

I gasp as I click the phone off and throw the phone away from me.

My heart stops beating and a knot tightens in my stomach.

He hopes this is enough for me? For what…to break my heart?

To break *me*?

As if I haven't been living out my worst nightmare, he thought this was a good way to put the final nail in the coffin that was us?

I must be mistaken.

With trembling fingers, I pick my phone back up and play the rest of the message.

I start it over and hear the same heartbreaking words again. And then he continues. "I just have to know something. It's been eating away at me. How the hell did you find all this out?"

"It was easy," her voice chimes in. "I've known the stuff about Tessa awhile." My blood boils as I continue to listen, and I hold my breath as I wait for his reply to her words that she wants to get back together with him.

"I want that, too. I want to be with someone I trust, and you've proven that I can trust you."

My brows dip at his words.

Wait.

What?

He can *trust* her? After everything she's done, he *trusts* her?

"You...you do? You want to get back together?" She sounds as surprised as I feel...if that's even possible.

"It'll take some work, but the charity event, and lunch today—they're leading us somewhere, you know? You just keep proving I can trust you, okay? That's what's going to make this work." Something doesn't sit right with me about his words. Why would he send this to me? It's not like him to purposely hurt anybody this way, let alone *me*, the person he claimed to love more than anybody else in the world. I guess things change.

I hear some glasses clink before Savannah speaks again.

I listen as she tells him about a nurse at the hospital where I gave birth all those years ago. The knot in my stomach twists tighter as I listen to how she got her hands on the sealed adoption paperwork. It's sickening. It's hurtful. It's disgusting.

It's illegal.

An idea sparks in my mind.

"Thanks for all you did to help me." His voice is flat. Emotionless.

Unaffected.

The recording ends there.

I know him.

I fucking *know* him.

He would *never* get back with Savannah. Not after everything she did.

Was he trying to give me evidence against her? Maybe he sent this to me by mistake, and my first instinct upon hearing his words—especially his words against me—was that he was trying to hurt me.

But he would *never* do that.

He's getting close to her to get the truth out of her. If she can't see that, she really is as delusional as we feared she might be.

And she's falling right into his trap…which is perfect, actually. I have a gut feeling Tristan knows what he's doing.

I'm not sure how to respond, but I save the recording and forward it to Richard Redmond, whose number I still have programmed into my phone.

Me: *Tristan may have sent this to me by mistake. I thought you should have it.*

And then I wait.

I debate asking Sue for the millionth time to let me take a peek at the adoption papers, but something stops me every time.

I feel like it's something Tristan and I should do together…assuming, of course, he hasn't already looked at them and gotten in touch with the child's parents.

And so I focus on the baby and on the tasks Ellie has been sending me. She's keeping me busy, which is very much appreciated as I near the final weeks of my pregnancy.

My mom and I set up a small nursery in the corner of my room. I'm still not sure if I'll live in the house on the corner or if I'll be staying with my mom. I'm still not sure whether I'll move to Vegas or stay in Fallon Ridge. The more time that passes without contact from Tristan, the more I assume I'll stay here.

As much as that breaks my heart, that strange voice recording he sent to me today somehow gives me hope. He's got a plan in motion, and even if it doesn't end with the two of us together, hopefully it will end with Savannah facing the consequences of her actions.

Or, you know, maybe she could just…drive off a cliff.

CHAPTER 14

Tristan

It's risky, but it's my one shot.

It's a Thursday night, and I'm at Savannah's house. It's my first time here, and I don't know what funds she's using to pay for this place, but I'm guessing it's either a friend's place or it's paid for with money that doesn't belong to her.

She's got her hands in a lot of different illegal activities, but she's smart. She had both Jack and Luke Dalton paying her off for years and years, so maybe she invested some of that money to live the lifestyle she wants.

Or maybe she's committing other illegal activities to come by the money to pay for a place like this. I wouldn't doubt that for one hot second.

Unlike the Dalton brothers, at least I've managed to keep my money in my own account—for the most part, minus the legal fees Richard Redmond is getting from me that involve her.

Well worth the expense, by the way.

She's popping popcorn that she's never going to get to eat, and I'm pretending to drink a glass of whiskey I haven't touched yet as nerves light up my chest and my eyes dart toward the clock.

One more minute.

And then, right on cue, the doorbell rings, and my heart stops.

This is it.

We've planned the last two weeks for this moment.

I've faked my way back into her life. I've pretended I've been warming up to her, to the idea of us again. I've put on quite the performance, and right now is the payoff for all of it.

Her brows dip as she glances over at me, and she shrugs as she makes her way to the door. I stand and walk behind her because fuck if I'm missing a front row seat to this party.

She opens the door, and two police officers stand there. "Good evening, gentlemen," she says, immediately turning on her weird brand of sultry charm. "What can I do for you?"

"Savannah Buck?" one of the says.

She nods.

"You're under arrest." He twists her around and cuffs her, and I can't think of a more satisfying moment in my entire relationship with her.

Her eyes are wild as they find me, and I must be smirking without even realizing it.

She turns a glare on me. "You," she hisses. "You did this."

I laugh. "No, Savannah, *you* did this. And it's time you finally pay for all of it."

"What are you arresting me for?" she shouts at the officers.

"There are a multitude of charges against you, ma'am," one of them says. "But we're arresting you today on charges of extortion."

My jaw slackens as the word hits my ears and my brain takes a second to understand it.

Wait…*extortion*?

Breaking probation, sure. Blackmail, bribery, stealing court documents, yes, yes, and yes.

But extortion?

I guess it's one step further than blackmail. Does she literally have zero conscience?

The police officers haul her away, and I watch as they place her in the back of their car and recite her rights to her.

Her eyes are on me the entire time. They move from angry to pleading, as if I can jump in and save her from this…but I've been manipulated quite enough by this woman.

The officers close the door and drive away, and I watch the car until it turns the corner. I'm half-tempted to follow them all the way to the station just to ensure she's actually taken there.

I head inside, turn off the television, shut off the lights, lock the front door, and click the garage button before I run out, making sure it's closed behind me before I drive away, sagging into the driver's seat of the car I rented with a hearty feeling of relief.

It's done.

I have no idea what comes next for her. Prison time, hopefully. Fines, probably.

I decide to call Richard on a whim, and he picks up right away. "Is it done?"

"It's done. They took her in on charges of extortion. Know anything about that?"

"I do. Some of it is confidential, but new information came to me earlier today, and I acted quickly. Combined with the photos you sent me when you were looking for evidence on her, she'll go away much longer with this extortion case than she would have with our blackmail charges," he says. "There are twenty-three counts against her."

"What about stealing the records?" I ask.

"It's Chicago's jurisdiction, so if they press charges, it'll be handled separately. But extortion while you're on probation isn't a good look. With twenty-three charges at two or three years apiece…" He trails off.

"Do you really think she'll get forty or fifty years?" I ask.

"Nah," he grunts. "She'll be found guilty, sure, but she'll go away maybe ten, fifteen years max."

"Thanks for all your help, Richard." My simple thanks can't express how thankful I am, but the check I have to write him to pay my bill sure will.

"Any time, Higgins. Stay out of trouble, okay?" he says, and I chuckle.

"Will do. Keep me updated if you hear anything. I'm catching the red eye back to the Midwest." I pull into Travis's driveaway and cut the engine.

"Safe travels. You'll be the first to know when I get word."

"Thanks." We end the call, and I have to remember to send Jack Dalton a thank you card for hooking me up with the best lawyer in Vegas.

I head inside Travis's place.

"It's done?" he asks, standing when he sees me.

I nod, and he walks over, pounding me with a soft fist on the back.

"Congratulations, man."

I give him a bro hug. "Thanks. For everything, man. Seriously. It's been a strange few weeks, but I appreciate you opening your house to me even though I wasn't always quite myself. And all the whiskey, of course."

He laughs. "The door's always open, but maybe BYOB next time, yeah?"

I grin, an idea already formulating in my mind of sending him a pallet full of whiskey along with a subscription to some whiskey of the month club. I'll pull it up while I'm at the airport waiting for my flight.

We say our goodbyes, and he tells me to go get my girl.

I don't know what's waiting for me back in Iowa, but I do know one thing.

It's time to go home.

CHAPTER 15

Tessa

I can't get comfortable in my bed. It's three thirty-seven, and yet again, I can't freaking sleep.

I'm too close to the finish line.

It's raining, and the first drop of rain against the window woke me. I hear the occasional rumble of thunder off in the distance as the rain picks up.

I'm officially nine months pregnant now, and although I mostly feel pretty good given the fact that I'm close to pushing a watermelon out my vagina, my lower back aches and my hips burn every time I lay down.

I've taken to sleeping sitting propped up, but it's usually only good for an hour or two at a time. Thank goodness for the neck pillow my mom surprised me with last week along with the pregnancy pillow I keep stuffed between my legs.

And speaking of stuff between my legs…I'm freaking horny as hell. I've basically been having a love affair with my detachable shower head. I turn up the pressure as high as it can go and let it work its magic.

My mom asked me if I really need to shower two to three times a day, and the answer is a resounding *oh God yes*.

I really hope nobody checks my browser history, because I've been searching the weirdest things lately.

Is horniness normal during the last month of pregnancy?
Apparently yes, it is.
Is it okay to shoot water at your clit while pregnant?
No worries there.
Tristan Higgins.
No news.
I blow out a breath.

God, I miss him—and not just because I'm horny, though he would definitely know ways to satisfy those particular needs.

I miss having him next to me. I miss grabbing his hand and putting it over my stomach when baby girl kicks. I miss sitting on the scenic overlook by the river, holding his hand and resting my head on his shoulder as we take deep breaths together.

I miss dinners together where we talk about nothing and everything, and I miss binging our shows. I still don't know if Jamie made it out okay since we left off on a cliffhanger with the last episode we watched of *Outlander*. I miss dancing in the kitchen by the flickering light of candles, and I miss him being there when I go to dinner at his parents' house.

They've both granted me their forgiveness, for which I'm eternally grateful. It was Sue who seemed to really understand, and it was only when I admitted how much I hated my father for what he'd done that she told me the truth about him—and why she drifted from my mother for a short time.

He'd propositioned her not so long ago. She'd declined.

He didn't know how to have female friends, and what he did cost him one of his closest friends in Russ.

If anything, the fact that he did that to her only helped her understand what position he put me in when I was just a teenager. While I admit I could've handled things differently once Tristan and I reconnected, she seemed to understand that I was in a position where I couldn't change anything anyway. I was protecting Tristan, protecting our connection, protecting our friendship, protecting myself and my baby.

I'm grateful they're on my side, and I'm still hopeful one day Tristan will come around, too.

I pray for it every night before I go to bed. I was raised to say my prayers, and I always start by asking for forgiveness, particularly since I'm very aware that I'm not without faults.

I pad through the house, down the hallway, through the family room, and to the kitchen for a glass of water. The walk helps loosen up my hip, and it's when I'm enroute back to my bedroom that a bright light flashes through the front window. I glance toward the source, thinking it's lightning at first, but then a car pulls up and the back door opens.

A man steps out, and I squint, sure my eyes are deceiving me. I'm half-asleep. I'm dreaming. I step closer and closer to the window until I can clearly see outside.

Maybe I'm hallucinating…or maybe it really is him.

His head is ducked down as the rain beats on him, and he turns to say something to the driver, who speeds off a few beats later. My nose is practically pressed against the glass as I watch his every move, and when he turns back around, his eyes lift in my direction—maybe out of habit, maybe out of curiosity, or maybe out of the same burning need I feel for him.

It's him. He's really back.

He stares at me a beat through the window, and then glances at his parents' house before he looks at me again. The rain continues to pour, making it hard to see him across the space especially in the dark. I scramble over to my door, unlocking it and opening it to stare at him from my doorway. I want to hurl my body into his arms, but I also want to follow his lead.

I walk outside into the rain, and he doesn't move. I take a step toward him, and he takes a step toward me, too. It's pouring out here, and the huge old t-shirt I was sleeping in—one of Tristan's old high school shirts that was big on him back in the day, too—is already soaked and sticking to my skin. I couldn't find comfortable shorts, so I went without. I'm standing in the rain in a wet shirt and panties as I pray he came home for me.

When we're close enough that I can smell him—or maybe that's just the heightened sense of smell (also normal, according to my internet search), we're still way too far away from each other.

He drops his duffel bag, and then he practically rushes at me, tackling me into a hug the best he can, and his lips collide down to mine. The rain pours down over us, the droplets from his hair falling onto my face and mingling with my tears as he kisses me. It's messy, with teeth clashing and tongues tangling as we hold each other as tightly as we can. His mouth is everywhere at once and yet it's somehow not nearly enough as I clamor to get as close as I can to him. Parts of it are reminiscent of our first kiss on the football field in the rain after Homecoming, but we're grown now. This is an adult kiss, and nothing proves that more than the way his hand drags slowly along my torso.

I can only pray this means it's another new beginning for us.

It *feels* like a new beginning.

A chill in the air would normally make me shiver from the rain, but I'm warm in his arms. I don't care that it's raining. I don't care that we're both soaked through and freezing cold.

All I care about is the fact that he's here.

He pulls back, then presses one more kiss to my mouth before he leans his forehead to mine. "I love you," he says softly.

The tears fall harder down my cheeks. "I love you, too," I whisper.

CHAPTER 16

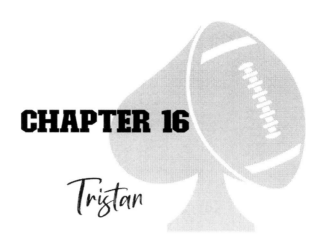

Tristan

I pull back and lean my forehead to hers. "I'm sorry," I murmur, oblivious to the rain falling around us. "I shouldn't have walked away, and I shouldn't have kept you in the dark. But I had to."

"I understand," she says, and she peppers kisses along my jawline.

I shake my head. She thinks she was giving me the space I needed to heal from her secret, and that's how it started.

But it shifted that night I went to dinner with my wide receiver brothers after OTAs. It became about clearing away the past so we could head into the future together. It became about making sure Savannah would get what's coming to her, and the only way I could do that was to fall off Tessa's grid.

I had to make Savannah believe I was all in on her again. I had to make her believe it was truly over between Tessa and me. It was the only way she'd let down her guard long enough for me to get the inside track, and once I knew where she lived, once she started spilling secrets…the rest all just fell into place.

There will be time to tell her that. Time to make confessions. Time to contact the adoptive parents if we decide together it's what we want.

But now…now's the time for a reunion.

"Come on in," she says, her arms around me as I clutch her as close as I can.

I realize the baby she's growing isn't biologically mine, but the second I saw her standing in the window watching me, my eyes flicked down to her belly as my chest warmed and that feeling of needing to protect both of them at all costs washed over me.

The baby is mine.

Tessa is mine.

These are my girls, and nothing will ever keep me from them again.

We're stronger than that. We're strong enough to overcome the secrets of the past. We're strong enough to hold hands into the future together. We're strong enough to get through anything, and it took Josh's words to remind me of that.

Neither of us moves after she invites me in for a beat, both of us scared to let the other go. She might be scared I'll run again. I might be scared she'll leave again. But neither of us are going anywhere, and we're long overdue for a talk about how we navigate this life together as we move forward toward our future.

I swing her up into my arms, carrying her like a child as I kick open the door she didn't latch shut behind her when she ran out here for me.

I lean down to kiss her, and she giggles. "Your duffel bag," she says, and I chuckle, too, as I set her down.

I run outside, grab my bag, and set it in the tiled entry to dry. It's soaked, but thankfully it's waterproof so the contents inside should be dry. But I don't care. It doesn't matter either way. I'm in Tessa's house, and she's standing two feet away from me, and as I reach out a hand to link my fingers through hers…that's all that matters.

I kick off my shoes, too, and leave my wet socks on top of them.

She squeezes my hand, and then she runs into the hallway and returns a moment later with two towels. She hands one to me, and I start with my hair while she wraps hers around her shoulders.

"Let's get some dry clothes," she suggests, and she nods down the hall. I grab a shirt and shorts out of my duffel before I walk quietly behind her toward her bedroom. The split floor plan means her mother's room on the other side of the house, and she's a fairly heavy sleeper, from what I remember, but I still don't want to wake her or worry her.

She closes the door behind her, and she rummages through her drawers to come up with a dry shirt and panties. She pulls off the wet shirt, and I can't help but stare at her body.

She catches me looking, and she blushes a little as she moves to pull on the new shirt quickly.

I walk over toward her, still dripping all over her carpet. I toss my dry clothes on her dresser and grab her forearm, halting her progress. I shake my head, and then I pull my own wet shirt over my head and toss it on top of her wet one.

She's in just a pair of panties, and I'm in just my shorts.

Her tits are huge and round, and her stomach has swelled even larger, and it's one of the most beautiful sights I've ever seen.

I missed this the first time around. Her father took these moments from us, and I will not miss the remaining weeks that we have left this time.

I kneel down on the floor in front of her, and I slide my hands along the sides of her stomach. I press a kiss there, and her fingertips tenderly find my cheek. I tilt my head up to look at her. "Don't cover this up."

"I feel disgusting, Tristan," she says softly. "I'm huge and my lower back is killing me and I haven't slept more than an hour at a time in weeks."

I push to my feet, and I grab her hand and walk her over to the bed. She sits on the edge, and I stare down at her.

I don't want to negate her feelings. She has every right to feel how she feels, but I want her to know how I feel, too.

"You are gorgeous. You are powerful. You are courageous. You are nurturing. You are growing a human being inside your body, and I can't think of a more incredible thing you could do. You're sacrificing nine months of your life to create and nourish life, and then you'll be a mother." I shake my head in wonder of the whole thing. "And I don't know if you're emitting some strong-ass hormones or what, but I've never found anyone sexier than I find you right now."

It's true. This primal need to mark her as mine lies heavy on my shoulders, but if she's uncomfortable, or if she feels disgusting, or if she doesn't want that right now, I'll back down.

If she does, though, all bets are off.

Her brows dip a little doubtfully at me. "You really think so?"

I kneel between her legs and finger the edge of her panties. "I really do. I've never wanted to fuck someone more than I want to fuck you right now."

She raises her brows. "Mr. Higgins!" she says, a hand flying to her chest in total shock at my words, as if she'd be clutching her pearls if she was wearing any…or if she was wearing anything at all. "I thought you'd never ask."

I offer a sly smile, and then I stand, slide off my wet shorts and boxers, and allow my incredibly hard cock to prove just how much I want this.

Her eyes widen a little, and she licks her lips before her eyes move up my torso before finally connecting with mine. "Am I going to be punished again?" She bites her lip and raises a brow.

"The correct question is am I going to be punished, *sir*, but either way, the answer is no." I take a step toward her, my cock moving even closer to her face. "No punishments tonight, Tessa. I just want to feel you, to love you, to show you how much I need you." I sit on the bed beside her. "What's going to be most comfortable for you?"

"Probably either me on top or you coming in from behind while I lay on my side. And I gotta tell you, Tristan, I've been so freaking horny the last few weeks. My shower head has been getting quite the workout."

My brows arch as I let out a little groan. "Goddamn, woman. Are you trying to make me come before I even get inside you?"

She giggles, and I lay back. She climbs over the top of me, and this might be the best view I've ever had during sex before. I reach down to line up my cock with her pussy, and she sits down, impaling herself on me.

We both let out low moans at the feeling, and then I slide my hands under her ass. I watch her tits as they bounce and sway while I penetrate her, allowing her to control the speed and depth to give her exactly what she needs. Her eyes move to mine, and I fight to hold on a little longer. I don't want this to end. I know we can do it again tomorrow, and the next day, and the next, but this reconnection between the two of us is unlike anything I've ever experienced.

It's the physical act, of course—the way her pussy tightens over me, the sounds of skin slapping against skin and the moans she makes when I touch her nipples paired with the taste of them when she lowers one into my mouth.

But it's the emotions that combine with the act that make this particular time with her so meaningful. Something passes between the two of us this time that tells me we finally got it right. We're finally bared to one another with all secrets out in the open, and neither of us holds back as we touch and kiss each other and do everything to show the other one how deep our feelings run.

And it's in that feeling that I arch into her, my body losing control as I start to come. The pleasure rips through me, and as I pump wildly into her from the bottom, she finds her release over me, too. She cries out when she comes, her climax tearing through her body as her pussy milks my cock for everything he's got.

When it's all over, she gently lifts off me and lays beside me, her head on my chest and my arm around her, stroking her shoulder mindlessly.

"Was that the best ever or am I just a horny pregnant woman?" she murmurs sleepily.

"Best ever."

We lay together a few minutes, and then she uses her body weight to push to a stand as she sort of waddles toward the bathroom to clean up.

I lay in bliss a few minutes as I think about everything we've been through to get to this moment.

It hasn't been easy.

It hasn't been a short road, or a straight path, or a simple route.

But that's what makes me believe that this time, we're going to make it last.

CHAPTER 17

Tessa

"I can't sleep," I say after I've used my full body weight to change sides three times. I've been trying to fall asleep for the last hour, but it's useless.

"I can't, either," he murmurs in the dark.

He normally wouldn't stay in my bed with me all night, but he didn't want to wake his parents, and with the rain…I told him to just stay.

"Sorry. Is it because I keep moving around?" I ask.

"Not at all. It has more to do with being wired after drinking coffee on my flight back and then the adrenaline rush of the workout you just gave me." He sits up.

I chuckle as I sit up, too, and I swing my legs over the side of the bed. "Doesn't sex usually make men sleepy?"

"Not when your heart gets pumping the way you just did to me."

"Sorry not sorry," I say. "Want some hot chocolate?"

"More caffeine?" He shrugs. "Great idea."

We head to the kitchen, and I make us each a cup. We sit across the table from each other, and he blows into his cup in an attempt to cool the liquid.

"Can I ask you a question?" I begin.

He nods.

"What changed?"

His brows dip as he glances up at me. "I realized you were in a tough spot. I hadn't really put myself in your shoes until I was sitting at dinner with the other wide receivers and the story just came tumbling out. I realized you were doing exactly what I asked you to do. I told you not to bring up the past. I told you it didn't matter. I told you to focus on the pregnancy." He lifts a shoulder. "I told the guys how I wasn't sure how I could ever trust you again after you'd kept such a huge thing from me, and they asked me whether you'd ever done anything else to break my trust. When I really thought it through, the answer was no."

We're both quiet as he stares into his cup, and I stare across the table at him. I'm not sure what to say to that.

"I kept coming back to that conversation in my mind, and that was when something shifted. I knew I had to get Savannah out of the picture, so that was my next move," he says, and his eyes lift to mine. They're full of something—a strange mix of regret and warmth.

"Out of the picture?" I repeat, and then I lower my voice. "Did you drive her off a cliff?"

He laughs. "I was tempted, believe me. Travis mentioned that, too. But no. Instead, I put on the performance of my life, pretended like I wanted to be with her again, got close to her, got her to confide things in me…and then I sent it all to my lawyer, who worked his magic."

My brows arch. "Oh my gosh! That's what that was!"

"What what was?" he asks, clearly confused.

"You texted me an audio file. At first when I listened I thought you were trying to hurt me, to put that final end between us, but then I realized you would *never* handle things that way. I figured you sent it to me by mistake, and I forwarded it to your lawyer."

His brows dip. "Wait…what?" he slides his phone out of his pocket and looks at his last text to me. "Why didn't you say anything?"

I shrug. "I knew you'd get in touch with me when you were ready." Baby girl kicks, and I set a hand over my stomach. "I knew you'd come back for us."

"Is she kicking?" he asks.

I nod, and he rushes around the table to set a hand on my stomach. I set my hand over his, and after everything that's gone down over the last few months, I finally feel at peace.

She quiets down, and Tristan returns to his seat. He looks into his cup again, avoiding my gaze. "So you heard me say that you lied and manipulated, and you still chose to believe the best in me?" His eyes flick up to me at the end of his question, and I nod.

"I will always believe the best in you, Tristan," I say softly, and I can't believe how true those words are.

I feel…healed.

I'm still hurt over what my father did. I'm still hurt over the way Cameron treated me.

But with Tristan, I'm whole again. With him, I can handle the hurt because he's there to help me through it.

He reaches across the table and squeezes my hand. "I'm sorry I didn't tell you what I was doing with her. I'm sorry I got scared and chose to run from you. I won't do that again. Ever."

"You did what you had to. I chose to have faith that it would all work out in the end, and you're sitting across from me drinking hot chocolate at four-thirty in the morning. I'd say it all worked out." I take a sip of my drink.

We talk about our time apart, and we talk about our history, and we talk about our time together, and a little after five-thirty, my mom saunters into the room. She freezes and her eyes widen when she spots Tristan sitting at the table across from me, and then her face breaks out into a grin.

"I knew you'd be back," she says, and she messes up his hair.

He laughs. "I knew I would be, too. Just needed to take care of a few things first."

"And?" she asks, and I realize then that in our conversation over the last hour, he never told me how things panned out with Savannah.

"My ex-wife was taken into custody last night, and my lawyer will keep me updated on the case," he says.

I gasp. "She was taken into custody?"

"She's done stealing records, blackmailing, and bribing," he says. "I gave everything I had to Richard, and we called the police with our evidence. I guess Richard came into some news at the last hour, because when they arrested her, it was on twenty-three counts of extortion."

"Extortion?" my mom and I say at the same time.

"I don't know many details, and I'm not sure I care. She broke the terms of her probation with some pretty serious charges, and I'm thrilled she's finally going to get what's coming to her," he says. "Oh, that reminds me. I need to call Luke later and tell him. He and Jack will be thrilled, too, and I'm sure they'd be happy to testify against her if it comes to that. But my guess is that it won't."

"Do you think she'll plead guilty or not?" my mom asks.

He shrugs. "Knowing her, she'll do whatever she can to spin it on someone else. But twenty-three counts of extortion seems pretty serious to me. I'm not sure she can spin that one."

"Well whatever happens, we're glad to have you back, Tristan," my mom says, and she squeezes his shoulder warmly.

"I'm glad to be here."

She grabs a cup of coffee before she disappears to take her shower, and once she leaves for work, we head next door to say hi to his parents.

We ring the bell, and his mom answers. She practically leaps at her son, pulling him into a hug and kissing his cheeks. "I missed you so much. Are you doing okay?"

He nods and holds her tightly for a beat. "I'm doing great. Is Dad around?"

She nods toward the garage. "He's been working on some projects. He's been doing a lot better the last couple days. Says he feels about ninety percent himself again, which is a huge improvement."

We follow her through the house and out to the garage, where we find him standing with a drill, safety glasses covering his eyes. The drill isn't as loud as the saw at this early hour, and when he sees us, he shuts it off and sets it down.

He pulls his glasses off as his eyes shift between the two of us.

"Welcome home, son," he says gruffly, and tears heat in my eyes as I watch them hug.

CHAPTER 18

Tristan

We pack up our stuff and head to our house, where we make more hot chocolate, binge Netflix, fall asleep on the couch, and spend the day just being together.

It's as we're eating dinner—chicken and vegetables with brown rice that I whipped up, naturally—that she asks the question that's been looming between us all day.

"Have you looked at the papers?" The question comes out quiet, almost like she's afraid to ask.

I nod, my eyes wide at my admission as I chew some chicken.

"So you know his name?"

I nod again.

"Have you, um…have you been in contact?"

I shake my head. "No. My mom still has the actual paperwork, but she sent me photos of the pages. I thought about looking up the family on social media, but it felt wrong to do anything without you. It felt like something we needed to do together."

She nods. "Do you want to?"

"I don't know." I shake my head as I set my fork down. "I don't know what the right thing to do is. I don't want to interrupt his life if he's happy and thriving, but I keep thinking…what if? What if he isn't happy? What if he isn't thriving? What if we could give him a better life?"

"What's his name?" she whispers.

"Logan James Wesley." My chest thumps as I say his name, and saying it out loud does something strange to me. I trip over the words a little as I try to get them out, but I realize for the first time that it feels like a piece is missing from me. From *us*. From this home we're sharing. There are six chairs around our kitchen table, and a boy who's almost seven years old should be occupying one of them.

Her eyes widen. "What?"

I clear my throat. "Logan James Wesley."

"Oh my God," she murmurs. "In Chicago?"

My brows dip as I nod.

"Oh my God," she says again, a little louder this time. "I know him."

My pulse picks up speed. "You do?"

She nods as her fork clatters loudly to the table. "He was a patient!"

"He was?"

She nods. "Yes! His parents…they're wonderful. They're loving and supportive. I had no idea he was adopted, but he was one of those kids I always felt a special bond with. A great kid. Smart, sweet. Funny. No brothers or sisters, and he's the center of his parents' universe. He always picked cherry suckers and would take the superhero stickers after his appointments."

She's animated as she talks about him, and I can't quite categorize how that makes me feel. She knows him. She knows our son. She's met him. She's *cared* for him. She knows he likes cherry flavored suckers and superheroes.

But she never knew he was ours…and I didn't even know he existed.

"He sounds like a great kid," I murmur, not sure what else to say as my heart inexplicably feels both full and broken at the same time.

"I can't believe he was literally right under my nose the entire time." The color drains from her cheeks. "Oh God. He came in sick a few times, and Dr. Foster recommended he had more tests done. We went to the hospital to be with him…and then we bonded when we learned it was anemia and not leukemia."

"Anemia?" I repeat. "Our child has anemia?"

She nods.

"My mom had hemolytic anemia as a kid."

"That tracks," she says, and something in her tone is quiet—as if she's feeling that same sense of fullness and loss that I am. "Hemolytic anemia is hereditary. But I had no idea about your mom."

I lift a shoulder. "Why would you? It's never come up."

She nods. "I never heard from Dr. Foster what kind of anemia his was, only that the test proved it wasn't leukemia. Do you know if your mom's was mild or not?"

I shake my head. "I don't know much about it, but it seems promising to me that she's still here with us, healthy and thriving."

"Yeah," she murmurs.

A beat of quiet passes between us.

"What are you thinking?" I finally ask.

She sighs. "I'm thinking a lot of things. I'm thinking I want a look at his records. I'm thinking I want to know how he's doing. I've thought about him often since I left Lakeshore." She shakes her head a little. "I'm thinking we should get in touch with his parents and make sure he's doing okay."

"How do you think they'd react to hearing from his birth parents?" I ask.

Her eyes lift to mine. "I have no idea."

Neither of us finishes our dinner. Instead, we leave the plates on the table and head to the family room. It's seven o'clock, which likely means our son is still awake. I wonder whether we should hold off, but neither of us wants to wait.

I read the number from the photo my mom sent me, and Tessa dials it into her phone with trembling fingers. She glances up at me before she clicks the call button, and I nod as my heart thunders in my chest.

She draws in a deep breath and exhales slowly before she clicks the call button and puts it on speaker.

"Hello?" a woman's voice answers.

"Is this Miranda Wesley?" Tessa says.

"Yes it is."

"Hi, it's Tessa Taylor. Logan's nurse from Lakeshore Pediatrics?" she says, lifting her voice at the end as if she's asking a question.

"Oh yes, hello! Are you back at the practice?" she asks.

"Well, no—" Tessa begins to answer, but Miranda cuts her off.

"You were always his favorite nurse there. He's missed seeing you around."

"He was always one of my favorite patients," Tessa says, her voice cracking a little as she brushes away a tear.

I squeeze her hand in solidarity, and when her eyes flick up to mine, I nod my encouragement.

She nods back at me. "How's he been doing?"

"He's okay," she says. "Dr. Foster has been a great help in getting his hemolytic anemia under control, but lately Logan has been telling me how tired he feels again. He went to bed at six-thirty tonight when usually he stays up until eight or eight-thirty."

Tessa seems to stiffen at the mention of Dr. Foster. How that asshole could be such a good doctor and treat women like such trash a second later is beyond my realm of understanding.

"Have you taken him in for testing?" Tessa asks.

"We have an appointment scheduled next week, so I figured we'd do the wait and see thing," she says. "You think that's okay?"

"I think you should probably get him in as soon as you can if new symptoms are popping up," Tessa says. She sets a hand over her stomach and rubs it a little.

"Okay. To Lakeshore?"

"Yes," Tessa says. "You should be able to book right on the patient portal and get in tomorrow. Dr. Foster will likely recommend you to Children's, but better to be seen and get the ball rolling, you know?"

"Good idea," Miranda murmurs. "Thanks, Tessa. How have you been?"

"Great," Tessa lies.

"I'm so happy to hear that. Thanks so much for the call. I think this must be divine intervention because I was debating whether or not to have him seen sooner, and I'm going to get off the phone right now and book his appointment for tomorrow," she says.

"Sounds great. You have my number now if you have any questions. I'm happy to help," Tessa says.

I nudge her a little, but she just looks at me and shrugs. Her eyes bulge out a little as she points to her phone as if to ask me *how the hell do I bring it up right now* and I don't really have an answer for that.

I suppose I could always butt in with *hi Miranda, I'm NFL wide receiver Tristan Higgins, oh and by the way I just found out I'm your kid's biological father.*

Yeah…no.

And so we'll wait.
At least we have the connection now.

CHAPTER 19

Tessa

"I couldn't do it," I whisper after I end the call. I brush some tears away. "I couldn't blow up her world when she's worried about him. I couldn't make myself say the words."

"I understand," Tristan says. "It's a lot to say. We can take our time. There's no need to rush into anything."

I nod, not really feeling any better about any of this as he throws a bunch of clichés at me.

I'm worried about Logan, and it's like Tristan can sense that as he offers words to make me feel better.

"You helped. They might have waited if you hadn't called tonight," he says.

I nod.

Still, Miranda never asked why I was calling. I guess I started the conversation by saying I just wanted to check on Logan, and I did. I found out more, and I convinced her to take him into Lakeshore sooner rather than later.

And then I couldn't say the words.

I wasn't ready. I was scared.

It felt like something that should be said in person, not over a speaker phone at seven o'clock at night.

We wash the dinner dishes, and then we settle in for the next episode of *Outlander* at Tristan's suggestion to try to take our mind off things. To change the subject, so to speak.

But it doesn't help take my mind off anything.

It doesn't really seem like Tristan's paying any attention to the screen, either.

I can't stop thinking about Miranda's words. Logan has been feeling tired lately.

From what I know, hemolytic anemia can become aplastic anemia. It's not my specialty, but my mind is wandering and so my fingers are, too, as I do a little research on my phone.

What if it's aplastic anemia? What if it's bad?

What if he needs bone marrow?

Finding a bone marrow match can be tricky, but parents are automatic half-matches to their biological children, so if he did need a transfusion, we could potentially help him.

The timing would be awfully coincidental, but I'm a big believer that everything happens for a reason. Maybe Savannah really *did* do something good even though the way she did it was awful. But however she came by the information, we're in a position to help now if our little boy needs it.

I start to cry, and Tristan glances over at me as he hears me sniffle. He shuts off the television and moves a little closer to me. "Babe. What's wrong?"

"I just can't believe Logan Wesley is our little boy," I manage shakily through the tears that are quickly escalating into sobs. "I loved that boy. I always felt like he was special. I thought about him and worried about him but I knew he was in good hands with his parents and now…now…now—how could I ever rip him away from them?"

"Hey," he says softly, soothingly. "We're not ripping him away."

"But I want to be his mom. I want to take care of him. I want to be there for him," I sob.

He moves in beside me and pulls me into him so my head is resting on his chest. He rubs my back, and I hear a sniffle from him, too.

This is hard.

Really hard.

Baby girl kicks, and it's almost like she's saying *it's okay, Mama. I'll be here soon to give you a hug, too.*

I can't wait for that hug.

My tears finally calm, but I'm left with a wicked bad headache. I stand to head into the kitchen to take some Tylenol, and that's when it happens.

A splash of water down my legs, and then it sort of feels as if I'm going to the bathroom except…I'm not. "Oh my God," I yell. "I think my water just broke!"

Tristan's eyes widen as he looks from the puddle beneath me up to my face and back again, and then he springs into action.

"Are you having contractions?" he asks.

I shake my head. "Not yet."

He nods then runs to the kitchen and rushes back with two towels. He hands one to me, which I use in some attempt to dry my legs, and he mops the floor with the other.

"Do we go to the hospital?" he asks.

I nod. "I think so, but if contractions haven't started yet, I'm not really sure." And then the pain hits me. "Oh God!" I yell as what feels like the worst cramp of my life debilitates me for a second. But then I'm okay again. "I think they're starting."

"Do you have a bag packed?" he asks.

I shake my head, eyes wide as I perch on our brand new couch even though I'm soaking wet still. We can have it cleaned. I need to freaking sit. "I thought I had more time. Another week or two, at least."

"Can you walk up the stairs?" he asks.

"Yes, I think I can. No, wait. No." I shake my head. "Nope, I can't. Wait! I didn't unpack my overnight bag when we left my mom's. My toothbrush and essentials are in there. I just need some extra clothes."

"Do we have a birth plan?" he asks, and he's way too calm for the excessive amount of *uncalm* I happen to be at the moment.

"A birth plan?" I screech as if I've never heard of that before. "Hell no, I don't have a freaking birth plan! I know I'm supposed to, but I've been a little busy getting left at the altar and sulking! And I thought I had more time! I really thought I had more time!"

"It's okay, Tess. It's fine. We've got this," he says calmly. "You sit. I'll get your bag. What do you need?"

"An outfit to go home in. Non-maternity clothes. Underwear—one of my nursing bras and my maternity underwear. A t-shirt and yoga pants. And a dry outfit to change into before we go. I think I have one in my duffel bag, so just bring that back down. Oh! And the baby's coming home outfit," I say.

"The baby's coming home outfit?" he repeats.

I roll my eyes in exasperation. "Yes! The little outfit on the hanger on her dresser knob. It's washed and ready for her so we can take her home in it." He nods as he starts to walk away, and I continue barking orders behind him. "And grab my phone charger. And my good camera!"

I dial my mother as he races upstairs, and she picks up right away. "My water just broke!" I wail into the phone when she answers. I'm certain I just interrupted her game shows, but I think she'll understand.

"Oh, honey, how exciting! How are you feeling?"

"Terrified," I admit. "Oh Jeez!" I screech as another one of those cramps hits me.

"You've got this, my sweet Tessi-cat. Was that a contraction?"

"I think so," I say. "The last one was a couple minutes ago."

"Be safe, honey. I'll meet you at the hospital."

I can hear Tristan talking upstairs as he gathers everything we need, and I assume he's calling his parents, too.

I draw in a deep breath. "It's okay, Mom. I just wanted to let you know she's on her way. You try to get some rest since we have no idea how long labor will take, and you can come by once she's here, okay?" I hear Tristan as he comes toward the top of the staircase. "I better go. Love you!"

He leaps down the stairs, taking them two or three at a time, and he hands me an outfit—my favorite black maternity shorts and a t-shirt that says *June Baby*.

That's right.

My June baby is on her way.

CHAPTER 20

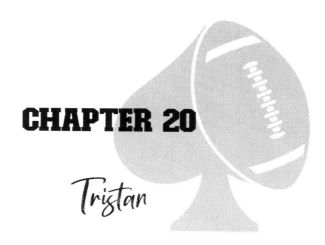

Tristan

I've always been attracted to Tessa, but the things she's doing right now…they're the most incredible things I've ever seen anybody do. Ever.

I'm holding her thigh up while a nurse holds her other thigh and a doctor looks between her legs. She's pushing as hard as she can to get the baby out, and holy hell is the female body an incredible thing.

"I see the head," the doctor says. "Push, Tessa!"

She pushes, and the baby doesn't come. She's been pushing for the last hour, and I can tell she's exhausted. She can't eat or drink anything, though, and she's a real champ as she keeps trying each time a contraction hits.

"And relax," the doctor says. "We've got about three minutes to rest and then I can feel it. She's coming."

In another three minutes, the baby will be here.

Tessa will be a mom. She already is, and she has been for both the last nine months and the last seven years. But she'll actually get to mother this baby. The events that led her here were partially out of her control, but she gets to make the decisions now, and the fact that she has decided that I get to be a part of her life and her baby's life means everything to me.

I will not let her down.

"Get ready," the doctor says, and just before I grab her leg, I lean down and press a kiss to her lips.

"You've got this, Tessa. I'm so fucking proud of you."

Her eyes fill with tears and she purses her lips as she nods once, a determined look crossing onto her face.

"Push!" the doctor yells, and she does with a mighty yell.

I try to watch everything—to see Tessa as she faces one of the many difficult challenges of motherhood, to see the baby as she slides from Tessa's body, to see Tessa's tears of relief and exhaustion and excitement as the doctor pulls the baby from her body.

That mighty yell is followed by the softest, sweetest little cry I've ever heard in my life as the doctor sets the newborn on her mother's stomach. The nurses flurry around, wiping the baby dry, and Tessa is staring down at her, watching her as she cries and draws in her first breaths of air in this brand-new world.

When she glances up at me, tears are in her eyes as she sees the tears in mine reflected back at her.

"Congratulations, mama. You did it," I say softly. I grab her hand, and she grips mine back, bringing it to her lips.

"*We* did it."

"It's time to cut the umbilical cord," the nurse says.

Tessa nods at me. "He's her daddy. He'll do it."

The tears that filled my eyes tip over, and I may be a professional athlete who walks into game day with my tough bravado…but if seeing my girl push a baby out of her body and then call me her daddy doesn't call for the happiest tears known to man, I'm not sure what could possibly top it.

I've always believed in love at first sight since I'm pretty sure I fell in love with Tessa the moment I met her, but this is a totally different feeling of the same concept. A wave of love rushes over me for this perfect, tiny creature. She may not share my blood, but she's definitely mine.

I snip the cord, and then the baby is moved up to Tessa's chest, where she continues to cry. The nurse brings blankets to put over the baby to keep her warm while she gets her skin time with her mama, and then the flurry of activity surrounding the birth starts to quiet.

The baby still cries as she adjusts to this bright, cold new world filled with air instead of liquid, but her cries start to soften as she slips into sleep. Tessa keeps her eyes down on the baby the entire time, and I can't stop staring, either.

"She's perfect," I murmur.

"She really is," Tessa agrees.

"Can I get you anything?" I ask.

"A cheeseburger and French fries," she says immediately, and I laugh. That's my girl.

"You got it," I say. I don't want to leave to go get it, and clearly the nurse sees my hesitation.

"I'll order one right up," she says.

After an hour, the nurses take the baby to weigh and measure her and do some other things, and I can tell Tessa feels the loss as they pull her away.

But we'll have time to hold her and love on her.

We have the rest of her life.

* * *

"Baby girl was born at four fifty-one AM, weighing in at six pounds, ten ounces and nineteen and a half inches long," I say, a little out of breath as I rush into the waiting room at nine o'clock the next morning as the grandparents have gathered. "And both mother and baby are doing amazing."

Janet hugs me first, and then my parents do, too. Everyone looks exhausted as they waited for the news, but I found that I just...couldn't leave them. I don't ever want to leave them again.

I know that's not realistic, but I also know that every time I'm not with them, they'll both be holding a part of me until I return.

"When can we see them?" Janet asks. She bounces on her feet a little with excitement.

"Now. I was sent out to come get you," I say.

"She's perfect, isn't she?" Janet asks.

I press my lips together and nod, a feeling of pride warming my chest. "They both are."

They follow me to Tessa's room, and I peek my head in first. "Ready?" I murmur.

Tessa's on the bed with our baby girl swaddled tightly in a blanket. She looks up at me and nods with a smile. She's exhausted after pushing a baby out literally less than five hours ago, and we didn't sleep much since apparently newborns like to try to eat every hour or so. Who knew? "Ready."

I wave the grandparents in, and Janet leads the pack. "Oh my goodness," she says, taking in her daughter holding her granddaughter. Her hands fly to her mouth as tears spill onto her cheeks, and my parents get choked up, too.

I draw in a deep breath and slowly exhale as I memorize this moment.

Our life ahead won't be without its challenges, but the feeling of *family* permeating this room is unlike anything I've ever felt before. This is one of those moments where we all have choices. I could walk away, or my parents could decide they don't want to support us...but what I realized today is that blood doesn't matter. This is my family, and it will be forever.

"What's her name?" Janet asks, and she moves to the side of the bed to get a better look.

"Fallon June," she says proudly, and then she glances over at me and clears her throat. "Fallon June Higgins."

"Higgins?" I say softly as I catch my bottom lip between my teeth.

She nods as tears fill her eyes. "Higgins," she repeats.

I can't help my smile. "It'll be your last name soon enough, too," I say.

She nods, and then the grandmas both go wash their hands so they can hold the baby while my dad shakes my hand and turns it into a hug.

"Congratulations, son," he says. "I'm so proud of you and the way you've stepped up."

"I love them both," I say simply, and he nods as if that explains it all.

And it does. I love them both. They're both mine.

Forever.

CHAPTER 21

Tessa

I've never been so exhausted in my entire life, but I've never been so happy, either. Tristan has been the perfect partner through the adjustments, gently but firmly helping me take breaks when he can tell I need them. A huge package came from Luke and Ellie with all sorts of baby essentials in it, and Travis sent a Vegas Aces onesie with Higgins and the number eleven splashed across the back.

It's hard to believe she's already four days old. We've only been home two days, and we're already taking her to her first doctor's appointment at the pediatrician she'll see when we're here in Iowa.

I haven't thought much beyond this appointment, to be honest.

I know we have just under a month before we need to go to Vegas, but the thought of leaving Fallon Ridge behind to move there with a newborn is daunting. We haven't even discussed it, but I can't imagine leaving my mom, of pulling her away from her granddaughter when she's already formed such a tight bond with her. Sue and Russ, too—they've been incredible, bragging happily to everybody about their new granddaughter.

We completed all the necessary legal paperwork to ensure Tristan's last name appears on Fallon's birth certificate, and he's officially her daddy.

And he's over the moon about it.

After we struggle to figure out how to strap her into her car seat in my SUV again, he drives under the speed limit the entire way to the pediatrician's office, and I can't help but giggle at him. He's nervous having her in the car, but I suppose it's something we'll get used to.

She's totally healthy even though she came a little early, and she's progressing nicely. I'm progressing nicely myself as everything down south starts the healing process.

And in four to six weeks, Tristan can explore all the goods down there himself.

I'm too exhausted to even think about sex right now, but with each day that passes, I start to feel a little more like myself again.

Once we're back home and the baby is in her bassinet napping after her appointment, Tristan joins me in the kitchen to help me make dinner. I'm chopping vegetables—green pepper, which I'm going to mix with onion and mushrooms to put on top of some shaved pork to make our own homemade Philly cheesesteaks, when he turns on some music. I finish chopping, and he grabs me into his arms as he Taylor Swift's "Begin Again" plays. We sway slowly around the kitchen, and when the song ends, he dips me then kisses me.

"What can I do to help?" he asks.

I nod toward the fridge. "Grab the pork while I get the veggies in a pan and slice the rolls so I can make them into garlic bread."

He nods, and we both get to work.

"How are you doing?" he asks me softly.

I glance up at him. "I don't think I've ever been more exhausted…or happier."

"Same, babe. Have you thought about Vegas?"

"A little," I admit. "I've been so focused on the baby, but I know our blissful time here at the house on the corner will have to come to an end soon."

"Our blissful time doesn't ever have to come to an end," he says. "I know I told you the Aces took my fifth-year option, and I feel good about my future there, Tess. I think we should start looking for a house in Vegas."

"You want to buy there?" I ask as I slide the veggies off my cutting board and into a pan.

"Yeah. There are some new developments going in close to the Complex," he says, and there's a new animation in his voice I haven't heard before. "It's not far from Luke's place, and we could look at spec homes, or we could build our own and put in everything exactly the way we want it."

"That's where you want to live?" I ask. "By the Complex?"

"Babe, you're not giving me anything here. What do *you* think?"

I can't help a little giggle at the nervousness in his tone. "I think we should do it. On the one hand, we don't really have a choice, right? You're going to be in Vegas the next two years at a minimum, with hopefully more. We can always come back here whenever we want to, and it'll be nice to have a home base wherever we are."

"Thank God." He wipes his forehead with mock relief. "I thought you were going to back out."

I shake my head. "Not back out, but I'm scared to leave my mom. She's been such a big help with Fallon, and I don't want to rip her away from her grandparents."

He nods. "I've thought about that, too. And that's part of why I love the neighborhood I was looking at. We have lots of options, but the houses they're building out there have connected casitas."

"Casitas?" I repeat.

"Like a mother-in-law's suite," he explains. "A little house connected to the big house. It has a kitchen, family room, a couple of bedrooms and bathrooms. You could customize it however you wanted, so we could add on one for my parents and one for your mom and then they always have a place to stay when they're in town."

"A place that isn't in our main house, so we still have our privacy," I say.

"Right." He slices one of the rolls. "And they'll have theirs, too."

"I love it," I say. "Let's do it."

"I'll do some research and get more information, and we can figure out exactly what we want."

He kisses me, and I can't help my little sigh of complete and total contentment.

The baby wakes just before we sit down to eat, and I feed her while Tristan feeds me. She falls back asleep, and I set her in a pack and play while we finish our dinner. We've already established a routine, and I'm loving every second as we adjust to our new life together. It just keeps getting better and better, and I can't wait to see what the future holds for us.

CHAPTER 22

Tristan

I've spent the last couple days in between helping with the baby talking with Kate Dalton, wife of Jack Dalton, the quarterback for the Vegas Aces. As it turns out, the neighborhood I was looking at is one of Jack's off-season ventures in real estate development, and his wife is the head of the design team. She has helped me create the perfect floor plan for our custom home, and as soon as the baby is back down after this afternoon's feeding, I can't wait to show Tessa the plans.

She's sitting on the couch with the baby in her arms, fast asleep. The television is off, and she stares at Fallon, a smile on her lips.

"Come look," she whispers when she hears me come into the room. I set my laptop on the kitchen counter and make my way over to where she sits in the family room. I sit carefully beside her so I don't disturb Fallon, and my eyes focus on her perfect little face, her rosy cheeks, her button nose, and her toothless little smile.

Wait…a smile?

"She's smiling," I whisper.

Tessa nods, a smile lifting her lips, too. "I wonder what she's dreaming about."

"Probably your tits. I know that's what I dream about."

She gasps with a soft laugh and shakes her head.

"For nourishment," I say. "Get your mind out of the gutter."

She chuckles again.

"I have some house designs to show you when you're ready," I say.

She nods. "I can't wait to see."

Her phone starts ringing, and it's startlingly loud in the quiet room. It's over on the kitchen counter, and I leap up to silence it before it wakes the baby.

I hand it over to her, and her eyebrows dip as she stares at the screen. "It's Miranda Wesley."

I take Fallon from her arms so she can answer, and I head toward the bassinet in the living room in the front of the house. We have baby monitors everywhere, so we'll hear her if she wakes, but she'll be far enough away that the voices won't wake her.

"Hello?" I hear her answer as I set Fallon down. I watch her for a few seconds, and she's still sleeping. I rush back toward Tessa, and she puts the call on speaker.

"How are you?" she asks.

"Worried," Miranda says. "We got the tests back, and Logan's hemolytic anemia has become aplastic anemia."

My chest tightens when she says the words. I don't know what aplastic anemia is, but Tessa's next words have me a little scared.

"Oh no, Miranda. I'm so sorry," Tessa says, and there's definite panic on her face.

"Dr. Foster says the only cure is a bone marrow transplant and I'm terrified. I've heard it's hard to find matches, and Logan is adopted, so his father and I might not be able to help him. We could try to appeal to the courts to unseal his adoption records and find his parents since Dr. Foster told me that parents can be matches, and I'm not sure why I'm calling you other than because you *know* Logan and you're a nurse and you just called not very long ago to ask about him and I'm praying you know how to move this process along to save my son." She starts to cry as she babbles.

Tessa glances at me, and I nod. She clears her throat. "I, um…I think we might be able to help."

"I knew you could. My gut told me to call you, and I knew you'd know what to do," she says, her voice trembling.

Tessa's eyes edge to me again. They're wide, and she looks nervous. I reach over and squeeze her hand in solidarity.

"I, um…I have something I need to tell you," Tessa begins. "I know who Logan's biological parents are."

There's silence for a beat before Miranda speaks again.

"You do?" she finally asks, hope apparent in her voice. But then it's like a switch flips as she realizes something, and the hopelessness and fear is back in her tone. "Wait…no. How could you? Those records…they're sealed. The birth mother wanted to make sure there was no way anyone would ever find out, it was all through this private agency—"

Tessa interrupts her. "I'm his birth mother."

Silence greets those words on the other end of the line.

The silence stretches into an uncomfortable amount of time.

"And I'm his birth father," I finally add.

Tessa's eyes connect with mine, and we share a look of understanding that means we will ban together to do whatever it takes to save our son…even if it means doing it from the sidelines. Even if it means letting him live his life without knowing us. Whatever keeps him happy and healthy…that's all that matters.

Tessa opens her mouth to speak when her phone makes a little sound and the screen goes black.

Miranda ended the call. She hung up.

Tessa dials her back, but she doesn't answer.

"What do I do?" she whispers to me, tears filling her eyes.

"I don't know." I shake my head a little as my heart pounds with fear.

Fear for that little boy.

We can help. I *want* to help. I know nothing about bone marrow donation, but I will become educated so I can help that little boy who needs us.

"Should I text her?"

I lift a shoulder. "Try it."

I watch as she drafts the text.

Tessa: *I'm sorry to spring that on you. I know what a wonderful mother you are to that little boy, and the last thing we want is to upset any of you or your lives. We can proceed in whatever way makes you most comfortable, but we are both here and willing to help.*

She glances up at me, and I nod.

She clicks send, and the message is obviously read right away, but a reply doesn't come.

We both stare down at her phone, waiting and wondering.

The baby's cry pulls our attention away from the monitor sitting beside us.

"I'll get her," I say.

Tessa clicks off her phone and slides it into her pocket. "Let's both go," she suggests, likely as a way to distract us from what just happened.

But there's no distraction from knowing your child needs you and there's nothing you can do about it.

CHAPTER 23

Tessa

"These are incredible, Tristan," I murmur. I look at the floorplan he mapped out for us. Over nine thousand square feet, six bedrooms, six bathrooms, a gym, a pool, and not one but *two* casitas—one for his parents and one for my mom.

It's more than the twelve-year-old with big dreams for the future ever could have come up with, and he's offering it to me.

And for real…not just in a dream.

"We could do this plan, which would be totally customized to what we want." He's standing behind me as I sit at the kitchen table, looking at his laptop screen, and he gestures toward the floorplan. "Or we could look at a few specs in the same development."

"What's a spec?"

"It's when the builder builds a home on speculation it'll sell. Sometimes they show up because deals fell through, but it's always a new home that's close to move-in ready," he says.

"So no customizations?" I ask, and he shakes his head.

"Most of the custom stuff would probably already be done, but we might be able to switch out some last-minute options."

"What's the difference in how quickly we could move in?"

He shrugs. "I'd have to ask Kate. A fully custom home would take longer. A year or more, most likely. But the specs could be ready tomorrow. Either way, I know Ellie would still love to have us stay with her if there's a gap between when we need to be there and when the house is ready."

"Have Kate send you what she's got in specs, and we'll start there," I suggest. "Maybe we can find one close to what we want and see what additions we can make."

"Good idea," he says. He pauses. "You doing okay?"

I lift a shoulder. It's been over twenty-four hours since Miranda hung up on me, and I can't shake the feeling that I need to try to get in touch with her again. "I'm okay. Fallon is keeping me occupied, but I'm worried."

"I know, baby. I am, too." He squeezes my forearm. "I spent some time looking up bone marrow donations."

"Oh?" I ask. I know a little about it, but as a nurse at a private practice, it didn't come up too often. "What did you learn?"

"I learned recovery is between one and seven days, and the marrow can be transported to the patient. So if Miranda is scared we're going to demand access to our son if we donate, we can tell her we don't even need to be in the same geographical area if I'm a match to him."

"And how would the Aces feel about you doing this?" I ask.

He lifts a shoulder. "It's not their concern."

"It *is* their concern, Tristan. You signed a contract with them," I remind him.

"I know," he mutters. "I'll talk to Adrian."

"We can both check to see if we're matches," I offer.

He shakes his head. "There's a recovery involved, and Fallon needs you."

"I feel helpless, though," I admit. "I want to do something."

"You did. You reached out to Miranda, and you're her point of contact with us. The ball is in her court now, but we can still be proactive." He gently massages my shoulders, and I tip my neck back as I give into the relaxation.

"Mm," I murmur.

"You better knock off those little moans right now," he warns.

I giggle. "Or what?"

"Babe, I'm horny as hell watching you be the woman I always knew you'd become, and I still have to wait *weeks*."

"My mouth isn't off limits," I say, and for a beat, silence engulfs us as neither of us can actually believe I just said that.

The massage stops, and Tristan's fingers sink into my hair. He gently tugs my head back, and my eyes meet his upside down. "Then open wide because I have a snack for you."

I giggle at his words, and my phone starts to ring at that moment, interrupting our intimate moment—and interrupting my thought process as I tried to figure out whether he was serious or not. I mean…I'm up for it if he is. I'm feeling more like myself every day as I settle into this new life, which is about to get flipped upside down in another few weeks when we move to Vegas.

He grabs my phone off the counter for me, and he hands it over to me.

Unknown Number.

I debate picking it up, and then some gut feeling has me swiping to answer. "Hello?"

"Is this Tessa Taylor?" the male voice on the other end asks.

"Yes it is," I say, laughing as Tristan makes a show of slowly unzipping his pants.

"This is James Wesley."

My eyes widen as I freeze, and Tristan senses my change in demeanor immediately as his brows knit together. I put the call on speaker so he can hear, too.

"Oh, hi," I say as I think of what I know about Logan's dad. I only met him maybe twice, but I remember how gentle he was with his son when he brought him into the office. "What can I do for you?"

He clears his throat. "Miranda…she's terrified you're going to take him from us, but I'm terrified we're going to lose him without you. I told her I'd rather keep him on this Earth without us than lose him to this disease. She agreed, but she couldn't move herself to make the call. So…here I am…to talk to you, to learn what happened, to get to know you, and to see if you can help."

"We're happy to help," I say gently. "And we won't take him from you. I know how happy and well-adjusted he is, and I know he must be terrified right now. I would never want to hurt him or you."

"Why did you call my wife a week ago?" he asks, ignoring everything I just said. Well…maybe not *ignoring* it, but tucking it away for later.

"I—I'm not sure," I stutter. "I guess I just wanted to tell her I was here if you needed anything."

"What happened? Why'd you give him up?" James asks.

I clear my throat. "I was seventeen and my father made me."

"But the ladies at the agency all said—"

"My father was very good at painting situations in whatever way most benefitted him," I say, interrupting him. "I didn't want to give up that boy, but he left me with no choice." I hear the pain in my own voice even though I'm trying to mask it. "And now…I just want him to be happy and healthy, and if there's anything I can do, or not do, to contribute to that, just tell me."

"And the baby's father?" he asks softly.

"That's me," Tristan says. "My name is Tristan."

"I know a little about Tessa. Tell me something about yourself."

Tristan glances over at me, and everything feels like it just got a hundred times more complicated.

If he tells them he's a football player, they can look up what he makes online fairly easily even though that's the base number and not the final amount that goes into his bank account. And then they might expect certain things.

The thought of them using Tristan for his money and stature but not allowing us to see our son presses a sort of heavy weight on my chest that I'm not sure I've ever felt before.

"Um…I'm six feet, five inches tall," Tristan says.

"So *that's* where Logan gets his height from," James murmurs.

"He's tall?" Tristan asks.

"Ninety-ninth percentile for height pretty much since he was born," James says, and a beat of silence follows that. They've been with him since he was born.

I birthed him and thought I'd never see him again…and then I did and didn't even know it.

What a tangled web.

It should have been us, but we can't change the past. We can only forge ahead. And I can tell Tristan is antsy to get to what comes next instead of standing here making small talk when he abruptly shifts the topic.

"I would like to get tested as soon as I can to see if I'm a match for your son," Tristan says quietly.

"We'd appreciate that very much," James says. "I guess…let us know how it goes. If you turn out to be a full match, we'll figure out where to go from there."

We say goodbye and hang up, the conversation weighing heavily in the room.

Tristan glances at the clock. "It's too late to do anything tonight, but I can go get swabbed tomorrow and start the process to see if I'm a match."

I nod, and I'm about to add more when my phone starts to ring again.

I glance at the screen.

Tiffany Gable.

I click it off, ignoring it, but Tristan saw it too.

"What the hell do you think she wants now?" he asks.

"I have no idea," I murmur, but I have a feeling we'll find out soon enough.

CHAPTER 24

Tristan

Tessa puts her phone on speaker after it dings with a new voicemail.

"Hey Tessa, it's Tiffany," the voicemail says. "I was really hoping you'd pick up, but I understand why you didn't. I just wanted to apologize. My behavior was…out of line. I'm sorry for hurting you. I'm sorry about the JustFans profile. I started seeing this new guy and he's really helped me open my eyes to my pattern of lying." She lets out a long exhale. "And by *new guy*, I mean a therapist. Anyway, Christian made me see how much jealousy I actually held against you. But that doesn't excuse my reaction. I won't call anymore. In fact, I'm thinking about moving out of town. Brandi offered me a place to stay with her in Vegas, so I might take her up on that. Okay, that's all I needed to say. Um…bye."

Moving to Las Vegas? Is she fucking with us right now?

And…*Christian*? As in…rhymes with *Tristan*?

What the ever-loving mother fuck is wrong with this chick?

Tessa exhales with audible frustration. "Oh for fuck's sake."

"What?" I ask.

"She's seriously moving to Vegas? I thought I'd be able to escape her when we moved there!"

I start massaging her shoulders. What a strange few minutes it's been. "It'll be fine, Tess. It's a big city."

"So big you ran into Brandi and Savannah everywhere you went," she mutters.

"Pure coincidence," I say, trying to sound convincing. I'm certain I fail. "But also, it would seem they were in search of me. They were going to find me no matter what." He pauses, and then he exhales. "Oh! That reminds me. Travis told me Brandi was kicked out of Coax."

"Coax?"

"The *club*," I say meaningfully.

She nods with recognition. "Oh? Why?"

I lift a shoulder. "The JustFans thing. She broke the NDA when she told Tiffany how she knew me, and that was enough for Victor to send her packing."

"Oh shit," Tessa says. "Brandi isn't going to be happy about that."

"Probably not," I agree. "But she's not our problem anymore."

"Have you heard anything about Savannah?" she asks.

I shake my head. "Not really. She pled guilty at the arraignment hoping to get a lesser sentence. Richard said she's on house arrest until her sentencing."

"Can you imagine her on house arrest?" Tessa asks.

I shrug. "About as much as I can imagine her in prison, which will undoubtedly come next."

"How does that make you feel?"

I think about that question for a second as I sigh. "It makes me feel hopeful that one more criminal will be off the streets and behind bars where she belongs." I try to remember the good times with her, but they were awfully limited before her true colors rang out bright and true.

The baby wakes, and it's feeding time again. She's already gotten into a routine, and while we're both running on empty after only getting two-hour shifts of sleep at a time, we've taken to giving each other breaks. I'll take back-to-back late-night feedings so Tessa can get a little extra sleep one night, and she'll take the next night to let me sleep.

And so go our days. I get my tests done for the bone marrow match, and it takes a few days until we confirm I am indeed a match. The baby is a little over two weeks old when I head to the hospital in Chicago on a Monday morning to donate my bone marrow. I could have done it in Davenport, but then it would have had to be transported. This way, fewer people are in contact with the product and Logan can get started sooner.

Tessa has been in contact with Logan's parents but only to let them know I'm a match and to let them know when my surgery is scheduled. They're very grateful but admitted they don't know how to handle any of this.

We remain patient as we allow them to suffer through this with their son. If they want us involved, we've agreed we will be there in a heartbeat.

My parents come with me to Chicago since I told Tessa to stay with the baby.

They put me under regional anesthesia rather than general at Aidan's recommendation, and it's weird that my body feels numb but I'm awake as they extract my bone marrow with a hollow needle driven into the back of my pelvic bone. After about ninety minutes, I'm taken to a recovery room. My hips are a little sore, but the doctors decide not to keep me overnight.

I head home a little worse for the wear but in good shape overall, and I keep my focus on the why. This will be much worse for little Logan, and if he can be tough and take the pain, so can I.

I just wish I could hold his hand during it. I wish Tessa could offer him cherry suckers and a whole truckload of superhero stickers. Because if anyone's a true superhero, it's the little boy who's about to undergo a bone marrow transplant.

Everything seems to happen in a whirlwind after that. My recovery is minor, and I'm back to normal after a few days. Tessa takes care of me and the baby, her true nature as a nurse emerging as she's tough on me when it comes to resting, eating, and hydrating.

I can't help but think she could put those skills to use for me when I'm in season, too. She helped get my bum hamstring back in working order, and I can see her being a great help to me as I face the weekly pains that come with being slammed into the grass by a two-hundred-fifty-pound cornerback.

I'm ready for our life in Vegas to begin. We've been packing up what we want, and after talking to Kate, we decided to buy one of the spec homes that had most of what we wanted. It was at a stage where we were able to add to it, so we'll still have two casitas and all the bells and whistles, plus Tessa was beyond thrilled that she got to pick out the flooring, countertops, and cabinets.

Although to be honest, I'm not sure if she was more excited about the house or the fact that she was discussing countertops with *Jack Freaking Dalton's wife*—in her words, of course.

We're driving since Tessa informs me we shouldn't fly with the baby until she's had her two month vaccinations, and we're planning to leave in a few days. It's a twenty-three hour drive that we're breaking up into a three-day road trip that will culminate at Luke and Ellie's house since our place won't be ready until November.

The baby is sleeping, which newborns seem to do an awful lot, Tessa is ordering things online to be delivered to Luke's place so we'll be all set up once we arrive, and I'm laying on the couch watching Sports Center when I hear Tessa's phone start to ring.

"It's Miranda," she says softly.

I click off the television and rush over toward her.

"Hello?" she answers, putting it on speaker so I can hear, too.

"Hi, Tessa. It's Miranda. I just wanted to let you know the transfusion went well. He's recovering, and there's a long road, but I'm already seeing him back to his old self."

"Oh, thank God," Tessa murmurs. I squeeze her hand.

"I…uh, *we* wanted to invite you to come see him. He's a real champ, but he was so scared going in, and I just know his favorite nurse will make him feel all better," she says. "And I'm sure he'd love to meet the hero who donated his bone marrow to help save him."

My eyes meet hers, and I nod maybe a little too enthusiastically.

"We've got a long recovery here at Children's. He'll be here another few weeks, so anytime you can drop by…" She trails off.

Tessa clears her throat. "We'd love to come by." She looks at me and shrugs, and I nod as if we're having some silent conversation. "We can come by tomorrow if that works."

"That sounds good," she says softly, and her tone makes me think she's not really sure how good it sounds even though this feels like the right thing to do. "Thank you. And we…um, we're not ready to tell him about the adoption."

"Of course," Tessa says softly. "Whenever you're ready."

They end the call, and Tessa falls into my arms as the realization seems to hit us both at the same time.

We're going to meet our son tomorrow…together.

CHAPTER 25

Tessa

I want to do something for them, but I don't know what. I tell Tristan that as he drives toward Chicago. Fallon is strapped in the backseat, facing away from us, and I've set up mirrors everywhere so I can stare at her precious face even though I can't see her. She sleeps soundly like she always does in the car, and I hope that bodes well for the twenty-three-hour drive ahead of us.

We're only stopping by Chicago for the day. We'll head back home, pack up what we can, and then start our trek toward our new life.

But this is an important piece of the puzzle, and I'm both nervous and excited to see Logan today. Nervous is definitely winning out, though.

"What about a care package?" he suggests.

"That's a great idea. What sorts of things do you think they need?"

He shrugs. "Meals, probably. I'm sure they're sick of hospital food."

"Comforts of home?" I suggest.

He nods, and we brainstorm a few more ideas and decide to stop at a store that carries basically everything from groceries and gift cards to blankets and pillows.

"Do you think we should make one for Logan, too?" Tristan asks. He's tentative—shy, almost, and it's the most adorable thing I've ever seen.

We fill the cart with all sorts of things like superhero coloring books, a squishy Captain America, markers and crayons, fidget toys, Lego sets, Hot Wheels toys—all things small enough to play with in a hospital bed, but also things I hope will brighten his days while he has to stay there. I think about throwing in a few cherry suckers, too, but he's supposed to avoid sugar during the healing process. I buy a bag of sugar free suckers anyway, deciding I'll keep them in the car just in case he's allowed to have them.

We grab two baskets, and I put everything together in the back of my car. A few minutes later, we're pulling into the parking lot at the hospital.

The last time I was here, it was to see the same kid.

A whole score of memories hits me, and it's like Tristan can sense it. He reaches over and takes my hand in his. "You okay?" he asks.

I rest my head on the headrest for a beat before I slide my head over to the left. Our eyes connect, and I spot the anxiety he must be feeling, too.

"Not really. You?"

He shakes his head, and I squeeze his hand.

"What are you thinking?" I ask.

"I'm nervous to meet him. I'm nervous that Foster works here. If I come face to face with that guy…" He trails off.

"I know," I say softly, and I glance toward the backseat. "But look what it got us. I don't forgive him, but everything happens for a reason."

He blinks as he nods, taking in my words. "I love you."

"I love you, too."

I text Miranda to let her know we're here, and she texts back to let me know they'll meet us in the lobby.

We get out of the car, and he moves to the seat behind him to grab Fallon's carrier while I move to the trunk to grab our baskets.

And then we head inside, my heart thundering in my chest the entire time.

If I'm nervous, I can't imagine what Tristan must be feeling.

I've met this child before. I've met his parents before. I know this family, and it's still hard for me.

This is all new for him.

I recognize Miranda immediately as we walk through the doors, and she's pacing nervously as she stares down at the floor. Her hair is greasy, probably unwashed as she spends day and night here at the hospital, and her clothes are wrinkled.

She glances up when she sees the movement of the electronic doors, and she freezes.

I do, too.

It takes Tristan's little nudge on the small of my back to force me back into movement, and I walk over to her.

"Hi, Miranda," I say softly. "Are you doing okay?"

She bites her lip, and then she breaks down into sobs. I set the baskets down on the floor and pull her into my arms, comforting her with a friendly hug as she cries.

"It's okay," I say soothingly. I'm not sure why she's crying, exactly—if it's because of what her son is going through, if it's because his birth parents are actually here. A combination of everything, probably, but in any event, I do what I can to make her feel comfortable in this moment.

She sniffles and pulls back from our embrace, and she nods. "I'm okay." She wipes away her tears and tucks some hair behind her ear. She looks over at Tristan. "I'm okay. I'm sorry. Hi, I'm Miranda. Your son's mother." She says it awkwardly as she holds out a hand, and Tristan grips it to shake it, still clutching onto Fallon's carrier handle with his other hand.

"It's nice to meet you," he says.

She glances down at the carrier. "Who's this?"

Tristan glances at me. "This is our daughter, Fallon."

"She's beautiful. How old?"

"Almost four weeks already," he says, and she looks away from the baby and back up at Tristan. I expect a question to come—for her to ask if this is Logan's full biological sister, but she doesn't ask.

"You're so tall," she murmurs, and he chuckles. "And he has your nose. Your eyes, too. Dark eyes but so expressive all the time." She glances over at me. "Tessa's mouth, though."

My chest aches as she says all the traits our son got from each of us. She knows these things about him. I've never had the opportunity to notice, not in the five minutes here, five minutes there I've had the privilege of spending with him.

"We got you something," I blurt in the silence that follows. I hand her the basket, and she looks it over then glances up at me.

"You didn't have to do this," she says as she brushes away more tears.

"I know. I just...I feel helpless." I lift a shoulder before I start crying, too.

"Please don't. You both have sacrificed a lot, and I know that. And you..." She looks over at Tristan. "You gave the bone marrow that is going to save his life. Neither of you should feel helpless."

The tears splash over my lids and onto my cheeks. "We, uh...we brought something for Logan, too," I manage softly. I hand her the other basket. "I hope it's okay. If there's anything you don't want him to have..."

"No," she says, looking it over. She presses her lips together as she looks back at me. "It's perfect. He will absolutely love these coloring books. This is way too much. You're too kind." She draws in a deep breath. "Are you ready?"

We both nod, but she doesn't budge from where she stands.

"He, um…we've never really talked about the fact that he was adopted. I figured someday we'd tell him, but at his age, it just hasn't come up. I'd like to wait until a better time. He's just…he's tired now, and he's recovering, and it's just a lot. For all of us," she says.

"We didn't come here today intending to tell him anything," I say softly. "We just wanted to visit and see how he's doing. To check on you and James, too. To see if there's anything we can do."

"Thank you," she whispers, and then she carries both baskets toward the elevator as Tristan and I trail behind her.

The elevator is awkwardly silent as we ride up together, and then the doors open. We walk down the hallway toward a room, and Miranda knocks twice on the door.

A moment later, James Wesley steps out. He shuts the door behind him. He looks much the same as the last time I saw him, but this time he looks like he hasn't shaved in two weeks and deep, dark circles mark the skin beneath his eyes.

He hugs me first, and then he glances over at Tristan.

And then he does a double take as recognition dawns.

"Holy moly," he murmurs. "You're Tristan Higgins."

"Tristan Higgins?" Miranda echoes softly, completely in the dark as to who he is.

"You're telling me that my son's biological father is Tristan *Higgins*?" James whisper-shouts, and none of us really know how to react to that.

"Well, who is he?" Miranda asks.

"He had over twenty-five hundred receiving yards with the Vegas Aces his first three seasons, and he was injured for most of one of them. He's caught over twenty touchdowns, he's been chosen for the Pro Bowl, he won a Super Bowl. Christ, man. You're Logan's *father?*"

He shrugs good-naturedly and shakes his head a little. "You're his father. I'm his bone marrow match."

Miranda starts to cry again, and I want to hug him for saying that.

"I'm a huge fan," James says. "I root for the Bears, of course. They're my hometown team. But I knew you were from the area. I always root for the hometown heroes, so to speak."

We don't correct him in saying he's really not from the area, but Iowa doesn't have a football team, so this is about as close as it gets.

"And, uh…Logan's a huge fan, too," he says softly, his voice full of pride. "Before the anemia diagnosis, he was out there running around in Pee Wee League. Then he started getting dizzy and tired all the time." He pauses and sighs, and it seems like the last few months have aged this man several years. "Anyway."

"Let's go in," Miranda suggests.

I reach over and squeeze Tristan's hand, and then we walk into the room together.

CHAPTER 26

Tristan

I see so much of myself in the boy reclined back on the bed that it's almost looking into a mirror of my childhood.

The shaggy brown hair. The dark eyes. The pinched brows. The big front teeth. The lanky body.

His eyes are focused on the television when we walk in, and his mom turns off the screen.

"Someone's here to see you, sweetheart," she says softly, and he spots Tessa first.

"Nurse Tessa!" he says. His voice is hoarse, and he sounds tired, but I still hear the enthusiasm in his voice.

"Hey, kiddo," she says as she moves over to kneel beside his bed. She's so natural with him, and I…I have no idea what to do. I have no idea what my place is here.

My heart skips a beat at the same term of endearment my parents have used for me my entire life.

"How are you feeling?" she asks. She hands him a superhero sticker, and his eyes light up.

"Tired, but better than yesterday," he says. "How much longer do I have to stay here?"

"I'm not sure, but I can check with your doctor," Tessa tells him.

"Dr. Foster has been such a godsend through all of this," Miranda says, and I nearly choke on my own saliva at the mention of his name.

Everyone turns toward me at the sound of my coughing. "Sorry," I mutter.

"Oh, Logan, I want to introduce you to the man who is your bone marrow match." Tessa nods toward me. "This is Tristan."

His eyes move toward me, and his jaw seems to drop a little. I think I spot recognition in his eyes, and for the briefest moment, I think he recognizes me as his father. But then, I realize that's not it at all. He recognizes me as a football player, and there's something hollow and sad about that.

"Thanks for the bone marrow," Logan says. "You look familiar."

I walk over toward the bed and hold up a fist for him to bump. He does it, and my chest tightens at my first real contact with the son I didn't even know existed until recently. "You're a real superhero, kiddo," I say softly around the lump in my throat.

"Wait a minute," Logan says, twisting his mouth dramatically. "Are you a baseball player?"

I chuckle as I shake my head. "No. No, I'm not. But I do play football."

"That's it!" he says with a grin, and if it wasn't for the fatigue in his eyes and the fact that he's in a hospital bed with a port on his chest, I'd almost never even think he's ill at all. "So now I have football marrow in my bones?"

That gets a good chuckle from around the room.

And then a thought crosses my mind. He already did have that football marrow in his body, and he doesn't even know it.

I wish I could tell him. I wish I could take this kid with me, be by his side during his recovery, be his father. I've got Tessa, and Fallon, and now the only missing piece from our family puzzle is Logan.

But even though he's ours, he's not ours to take. It's complicated, but part of the job of being a parent is knowing when to let them go.

I glance over at James and Miranda. His arm is around his wife's shoulders, and clearly they're facing this scary situation together, head-on. They're looking with pride at their son, and he smiles over at them with the knowledge that he's the proud owner of some new football marrow.

And it's that grin between parents and son that tells me even though it'll break my heart to walk out of this room, it's the right thing to do.

Maybe later we'll come to a point where we can meet again, where we can tell him the truth, where we can have a relationship with him...but right now isn't that time.

Miranda hands over the basket Tessa put together for him, and he pulls out every item with the excitement of a child on Christmas morning. He plays with the squishy Captain America toy—the one contribution I had to the basket—and then he starts to get sleepy.

James nods at me, and I take it as the signal. It's time for us to go. We haven't been here very long, and I don't want to go. I will *never* want to go. Tessa hasn't moved from where she's been kneeling on the floor beside him the entire time we've been in this room except for a minute when we sat beside him taking photos.

But it's time.

"It was great meeting you, kiddo," I say to him. "Tessa and I are going to take off so you can get your rest, but you keep being a superhero, okay?"

He nods, and he holds up knuckles. I bump my fist against his, fighting the urge to cry while I'm in here with him.

"You catch some touchdowns for me this year, 'kay?" he asks, his voice a little hoarse.

"You got it, kid. Every touchdown I catch will be for you. When you see me fist bump the camera after I score, that's my way of saying hi to you," I whisper. I can't put volume to my voice or the emotions I'm working so hard to keep inside will come spilling out.

I can spill them later. Not in front of the kid. Not in front of his parents.

Tessa leans down to hug him gently, and then she presses her lips to his forehead gently. "You keep getting stronger every day, you hear me? You take care of your mom and dad and just know I'm always thinking about you."

"Thanks," he murmurs as he starts to fall asleep.

Tessa stands there staring at him a beat. She presses her fingers to her lips, then touches his leg gently. I pick up Fallon's carrier, grab Tessa's hand, stare down at our perfect boy one more time, and then we walk out of the room.

Miranda and James follow close behind us. James shuts the door so we can talk in the hallway.

"That went well," James says, and relief is evident on his face. Maybe he was worried we'd try to take him with us or something. I wish we could.

"Thank you for inviting us." I reach out a hand to shake his. "If there's anything we can do, you've got our info."

James nods. "I appreciate that."

I get the feeling he won't use our info, though. He seems like the kind of guy who wouldn't just call me up for money. It's refreshing, to be honest, and I feel like whoever paired these people with the baby boy Tessa delivered seven years ago knew what they were doing.

"Dr. Foster is managing his recovery?" Tessa asks Miranda.

She nods. "He's been here every step of the way. He says engraftment is going well but we will need another week here at a minimum, so that basket of stuff you brought will really help us get through the next few nights."

"If you need anything else…" Tessa offers, and Miranda nods then pulls her into a hug.

"Thank you," she murmurs. She pulls back and looks beyond Tessa. "Oh, there he is now. Speak of the devil."

We all turn around to see who Miranda is looking at.

Speak of the devil indeed.

CHAPTER 27

Tessa

Tristan seems to crowd protectively over the carrier as we all watch Cameron Foster walk down the hallway toward us.

What did I ever see in him?

He's still handsome, I suppose, but he looks like he's aged since the last time I saw him. He's not the sexy, intimidating doctor he once was. Now he just looks exhausted, with dark circles around his eyes and wrinkles I never noticed before making webs near his eyes. He doesn't smile, and in some ways it looks like he's got a permanent scowl on his face.

It's only been about three months since the last time I saw him, but I'm sure Christine hasn't gone easy on him in those three months.

I wonder if he's still out banging nurses in his free time. I wonder if he's still lying to her about it. I wonder a lot of things, but I also don't really care. As much as I don't want him in my life in any capacity, I also know what an incredible doctor he is. I hate him, but he's caring for Logan.

His eyes meet mine first, and his brows dip together as if he's wondering what the fuck I'm doing here.

It's none of his business.

My immediate response is rage, but that seems to snuff out quickly. I don't need to be mad at him anymore. He served his purpose, and now he's in my past.

"Nurse Taylor, what a surprise," he says. He lifts his chin as he looks at Tristan, who stands some four or five inches taller than him. "And you are?"

Tristan lets out a strangled little chuckle, and I can tell he's barely holding it together. He wants to smash his fists into the good doctor's face, and I'm right there with him. "I'm Nurse Taylor's future husband and the father of her child. Oh, and Logan's bone marrow match."

At his description, Cam's eyes move down toward the carrier.

I suck in a breath.

Miranda and James have absolutely no clue that Dr. Foster is looking down at the child he helped create. The child he told me to take care of. The child he wanted nothing to do with so it didn't ruin his perfect reputation.

What a strange situation. Fallon's birth father is here, but he will never be part of her life. Logan's birth parents are here in the hall, wishing they could be a bigger part of his life.

Tristan protectively pulls the sunshade over the baby's carrier so Cam can't see in, and I stifle a chuckle. He doesn't deserve to see her. He doesn't deserve to know anything about her. He can fuck right off.

Cam raises his brows. "The father of her child. How lovely." A brief pause follows his words, and he opens his mouth to say something. But then he seems to think better of it and nods down the hallway instead. "Well, this reunion has been something. If you'll excuse me, I have patients to see."

"Of course," Tristan says, keeping the carrier to his side so he can keep Fallon protected as Cam walks past. "Hey, Dr.

Foster?" Tristan asks, and Cam turns around with raised brows. "Take good care of Logan. He's a special kid."

Cam nods, and his eyes edge over toward Miranda and James. "He's in good hands." He turns and walks down the hallway, and I suppose it's one thing we can all agree on.

We say goodbye to James and Miranda, who promise to send photos and updates, and James can't believe he has a real NFL player's phone number.

Then we take the elevator down and head out to the car. I feel like I'm leaving a piece of my heart behind, but I also know Cam was right. He's in good hands.

And that's just something I'll have to live with.

The ride from Chicago back to Fallon Ridge is quiet. Tristan focuses on driving, and I stare out the windshield as I reflect on everything that's happened.

Nothing has changed.

Not really, anyway.

We *know* now, so I suppose that's different in itself, but I still don't get to be with him. I still miss him and long for him. At least I know he's safe, loved, and cared for, and that's what really matters. At least that's what I tell myself.

"You're quiet," Tristan muses about halfway into the trip.

"As are you," I point out, and he nods, conceding.

"How do you think it went?" he presses.

I shrug. "About as good as it could have. It just doesn't feel right leaving him. You?"

"Same," he admits. "I saw so much of myself in him, it was scary. And the way you were with him...it was incredible, Tess. *You* are incredible."

Tears fill my eyes. "I didn't feel very incredible."

"We're doing what we have to do to keep his life as steady as possible," Tristan says. "It feels wrong, but deep down, I know it's right."

"It's like I know you're right, and in my heart, I know taking him away from the only parents he's ever known would be so wrong, so messed up. But I wish we could be selfish." I sniffle as I wipe away a tear.

"Me too. Someday, we'll get our moment with him. Until then, we have to just let him be happy and be loved. We'll do what we can from a distance." There's something in his voice that tells me he already has things in motion.

"Like what?" I ask, turning to look at him.

He clears his throat. "I may have paid off his hospital bills while we were there," he admits.

"Oh, Tristan," I say softly.

He shrugs. "It's nothing for me. Might be a pretty big deal to the Wesleys." He pauses, and then he adds, "And it's also why I'm planning to talk to my financial guy so I can set up trust fund and a college fund for both Logan and Fallon."

"Have I ever told you how incredible you are?" I ask softly.

He presses his lips together. "Not today."

I chuckle. "You're incredible. Thinking of the future for these kids…you're setting them up for success."

He's quiet a beat as he thinks over those words, and then he glances at me. "That's all I ever wanted to do as a parent." His voice is soft. "Set them up with the tools they need to be successful for the rest of their lives. Not just financially, but in every aspect. Emotionally. Physically. Mentally."

"You're the best dad," I say. "And a great man."

He presses his lips together and his mind seems to drift away for a moment before he glances at me once more. "I learned from the best." He's referring to his dad, and I couldn't agree more.

I wish my own dad had been more like him, but now I get to see Tristan as he fathers our children—both near and far—and I pray we'll be blessed enough to add more so I can continue to watch him flourish. He's a great football player, but when I see him with his kids, I know he's in the lifelong role he was born to do.

And I can't wait to watch him from the sidelines.

CHAPTER 28

Tessa

We pull into the driveaway of some huge mansion a little less than a week later.

I'm exhausted after three days in the car. Newborns are exhausting anyway, but traveling with one takes that exhaustion to a whole new level.

Between worrying about whether we have enough diapers and whether she's getting enough to eat and whether she's getting enough activity or if she shouldn't be strapped into her car seat for so many hours and oh then there's the thought of whether tearing her away from Iowa and her grandparents is actually a good idea…it's a lot to worry about for a new mom, that's all.

"Home sweet home," Tristan says softly as we stare at the house.

It's beautiful if not a little imposing as I stare up at it. "This is where Luke and Ellie live?" I ask.

"It's where we'll be living until November," he says.

I draw in a breath. How did this become my life?

Less than a year ago, I was sitting in a bar avoiding watching Vegas Aces games so I wouldn't have to be reminded of everything I lost.

And now I'm moving into a spare room at the Luke Dalton's house with Tristan Higgins and our baby.

What a whirlwind.

We grab Fallon, asleep in her carrier, and knock on the front door, and Ellie opens it a few beats later. "You're here!" she squeals, and she grabs me into a big hug. She hugs Tristan next, and then she glances down into the carrier. "Oh my goodness! She's precious! My littlest one is almost six months," she says, shaking her head. "Time really flies. Come on in."

Luke walks in behind her, and he's barefoot and gorgeous and I'm in freaking awe for a second that the legend that is Luke Dalton is walking around without shoes on and I can see his feet. Somehow even his feet are hot, and feet are about the least sexy body part to me.

And then I realize it's his home, and of course he's not wearing shoes, it all makes sense, but it still feels like I've entered some alternate universe.

This may take some getting used to.

Luke greets us, too—*with hugs*—and I manage not to faint as Ellie walks toward a staircase.

"Let me show you where you'll be staying," she says, and we follow her up.

She takes us to a huge guest room that includes a private sitting area outfitted with a crib and a rocking chair, and all the items we've ordered since we knew we were moving here are still in their original packaging, stacked neatly in the closet. The room has its own bathroom, and there's a window that overlooks the backyard. The view is gorgeous even at night. Palm trees surround the pool, and ambient lighting is set up to make it look like absolute desert oasis.

This is home for the next few months, and I'm so excited to get settled in.

Tristan brings up our bags while I feed the baby, and he tells me dinner's ready downstairs. Fallon's asleep, so I gently place her in the crib, make sure the monitor is on, and bring the other unit with me downstairs.

Everyone else is already gathered around the table, and when I say everyone, I mean…well, *everyone*.

Jack Dalton sits with his wife, Kate. On one side is a boy who looks to be around two sitting in a highchair, and between Jack and Kate is a little girl who looks about the same age as the girl sitting between Luke and Ellie. A little boy sits on Luke's other side in a highchair, and an older woman sits beside a man in a flannel shirt (yes, a flannel shirt in July in Las Vegas) and jeans. The sleeves are rolled up, and his head is bent close to the woman as they stare at one of the babies.

The doorbell rings, and I turn around as Ellie runs to see who it is.

She opens the door, and Ben Freaking Olson stands there. In his hands he holds two baby carriers, and a woman who looks a lot like Luke scrambles up behind him, panting as she says, "Sorry we're late!" to Ellie.

"No worries," Ellie says, hugging the girl. "Come on in and meet our newest houseguest. This is Tessa, Tristan's fiancée," she says.

"Kaylee," the girl says, and she gives me a hug. "Luke and Jack's little sister. Welcome to the chaos."

I giggle, and then Ben Olson walks in, sets down one of the carriers, and sticks his hand out to shake mine.

I nearly fall over from my knees buckling when he flashes his grin at me. God, he's even hotter in real life than on television.

The same could be said for my Tristan, though, and Ben picks up the carriers and follows behind Kaylee with the twin girls. He takes one girl out and sets her in a high chair while

Kaylee takes the other one out, and I slip into the empty chair beside Tristan as Ellie introduces us to the woman—her mother-in-law, Diane, and the flannel shirt man, who happens to be Ben's dad. I'm guessing these two are something of an item, and everybody here looks so freaking happy to be here.

It's chaotic, like Kaylee said, and it's loud as forks scrape plates and glasses clink together and laughter, so much laughter, fills the room. Babies chatter—and there are four girls here, all about the same age, plus two boys who are a little older than them—and the adults share conversation and I just sit quietly as I take it all in.

Ellie doesn't let me be quiet, though. She tells Kate how I've already started helping at her public relations firm, which gets a whole side conversation going about Prince Charming Public Relations, and I can't wait to really dig into my new job. It may not be nursing, but there are plenty of kids around here who I'm sure will keep me busy…especially those boys who surely take after their dads.

I always wanted the big family, and even though I found out about half-siblings later in life, that doesn't change the fact that we're still not a big family. I've grown closer to Stephanie, but we still have a long way to go until we're sisters.

This right here, though—this *is* family, and somehow Tristan and I have been accepted right into it without missing a beat.

I can already tell I'm going to freaking love it here.

CHAPTER 29

Tristan

"Was that too overwhelming?" I ask quietly as we slip into bed. I don't want to wake Fallon by talking too loudly, but she's in her little sitting room and I'm certain she'd sleep through it anyway. She's a good sleeper when she's asleep, and she's started going for three to even four hours at a time now.

She shakes her head. "It was perfect. They do those dinners weekly?"

I nod. "I guess they rotate whose house it's at, and this week it was Luke and Ellie's turn."

"That's so fun," she says. "It's just what I always wanted, you know?"

I nod. "Yeah. Imagine growing up with any siblings at all, let alone two of them."

"Imagine being Kaylee and having to deal with Luke and Jack as your brothers and the type of mischief they must've gotten into when they were younger."

I chuckle as I think to the two men I really admire. They've both taken to mentoring me, and I can't thank them enough—especially after I married Savannah, Jack's ex-girlfriend and Luke's ex-wife. Especially after Luke tried to warn me about her and I didn't listen. "They're good guys."

"I love those three women. They're all so welcoming. So genuine," she says.

"The four of you share a bond that not very many other women have." I reach over and take her hand in mine.

"We get to sleep with hot football players?" Her tone is anything but innocent, but she still hasn't been cleared for sex after giving birth.

I'm waiting not so patiently.

I'm also taking a lot of cold showers.

"You're all losing us to the game in a few weeks. Well, not Ellie anymore since Luke retired, but still. He's around a lot." I flip off the dim light on my nightstand then slide under the covers to get comfortable. "Did you hear him say he's coming to California with the team for consultations during camp? He's not coaching, exactly, but he's lending a hand. Plus he can work with the rookies he's signed to his agency."

"So he'll be gone, too?" she asks.

"Try not to sound so disappointed," I say dryly.

She giggles. "Are you jealous?"

I wrap a hand around her waist and draw her in closer. I press a soft kiss to her lips. "A ring on your finger letting the world know you're mine before I head off to the season would make me slightly less jealous." I buck my hips toward her, and she moans.

"Don't you dare get me going when I haven't been cleared."

I laugh. "Sorry. I miss you."

"I miss you, too. I'll find an OB tomorrow and make an appointment so we can get this show on the road. Are you serious about the wedding thing?"

She shifts subjects so abruptly I get a mild case of whiplash.

"Yes," I say. "I wanted to marry you back in May. It didn't pan out, but I don't see any reason to wait this time."

"What about the weekend before camp?" she suggests. "I should be clear by then so we can...um—*consummate*."

If the lights were on, I can guess her cheeks would be pink. I chuckle, and then I push her hip down and prove why I'm called one of the most agile wide receivers in the league as I hover over her half a heartbeat later.

She moans softly.

"I can't wait to *consummate* with you," I murmur.

"Maybe the baby can have a sleepover in Ellie's room that night?" she suggests.

"I think that's a great idea."

The next day, I get a call from Richard Redmond. Tessa is downstairs with the baby bonding with her new friends and I just got out of the shower.

"I have some news on your ex-wife," he says.

"Oh?"

"Her probation was revoked and she's been sentenced to twelve years—ten for the extortion crimes, two for violating her probation. It's unlikely she'll actually serve that long, and the judge was lenient since she pled guilty," he says.

"Thanks for letting me know," I say. Twelve years, or however long she ends up actually serving, isn't long enough, but it's better than her being free in the world to commit more heinous acts against innocent people.

When I head downstairs to tell Tessa, a look of relief crosses her face, but it's soured almost immediately.

"What?" I ask.

"I guess I just feel like we're safe until she gets out. But then what? Will she want revenge?" she asks.

I shrug. "Let's not invent things to worry about, okay? Maybe all the hard time will force her to take a look at her life decisions and stop blaming everybody else for what she's done."

"Maybe," she agrees out loud, but the tone of her word doesn't sound very convincing.

Still, I'm glad she'll be off our grid for however long she will be.

The next week is a flurry of activity. I head to the weight room with Luke, Jack, and Ben as if I'm a member of their extended family. Ellie set up a desk for Tessa in her home office, so she has a place to work, and their nanny, Elizabeth, is excited to have a newborn added to the mix. On a daily basis, she was already watching Luke's kids, Emma and Nolan; Jack's kids, Ava and JJ; Ben's twin girls, Hailey and Holly; and Josh Nolan's boy, Warner, who's around the same age as Nolan and JJ. Josh and his wife, Nicki, live literally across the street from Luke and Ellie.

It's a female-dominated group, but the three older boys still run the show, and poor Elizabeth is basically running a preschool out of the Dalton's home. Any more kids and they'll need to hire help for the help.

And in between getting ready for the upcoming season (me) and learning all about publicity (Tessa), we're planning a wedding on a very tight schedule.

There was an opening at the Cosmopolitan, and I grabbed it. I loved the Venetian, but there are too many memories there now to try a second time.

And so the Saturday before the Aces take off for California, I will wed the woman I love in the exact same place where Josh Nolan married his wife just a couple short years ago.

We'll be by one of the gorgeous pools at sunset, and I can't wait.

When Tessa is cleared for sexual activity at her doctor's appointment four days before the wedding, we decide to wait.

We've waited this long. It'll feel like we're both virgins again on our wedding night, and that sounds pretty fucking hot—

losing my virginity to the same girl twice in one lifetime. Taking hers twice in the same lifetime, too.

And the best part of all is that my dad has agreed—again—to be my best man. My parents and Janet are flying out so they can be at the wedding—again—but this time, Savannah won't be able to stop it since she's started serving her sentence.

I wonder briefly about Brandi and what she's up to, but she never struck me as strong enough on her own to cause any real damage. She fed information to Savannah, and she got kicked out of the club for it—a club that was a large part of her life. That might be punishment enough for her, or maybe she'll show up again.

Like I told Tessa, though, I'm choosing not to invent things to worry about.

Instead, I'm focusing on our future…and it's looking awfully bright.

CHAPTER 30

Tessa

I stare in the mirror as I try to push away the sense of déjà vu that's swirling around me.

Everything will be fine today.

I've repeated that line to myself no less than a thousand times since I woke up this morning. I really hope it's not a lie.

Everything's different this time around.

Different dress. Different hairstyle, make-up, manicure, pedicure, and shoes. Different feelings pulsing in my chest.

Aside from those things, I'm also a mother now. I was pregnant the last time we tried this. I suppose I was a mother in the technical sense before, too, only I didn't actually get to be the mom to my child. This time, my mom holds sweet Fallon while I prepare to walk down the aisle. I'll hold her as I walk next to my mom, three generations of strong women, and then I will vow my forever to Tristan with the baby beside us.

Neither Sara nor Stephanie could make it on the short notice I gave them, and so I've asked my mom to be my matron of honor. After I walk down the aisle, I'll hand Fallon back to her, and our little girl will be the closest person near us as we marry.

Luke and Ellie will be there, along with Jack and Kate, Ben and Kaylee, Josh and Nicki, Coach Thompson and Mama Mo, and Travis. It's only been a few weeks, but these people have quickly become our Las Vegas family, just as Tristan said they would.

It's a small event, but it's exactly what we want. After we're married, the staff will serve appetizers and champagne, we'll dance as the sun sets, and we'll be husband and wife.

Finally.

The day has gone smoothly up to this point, and I'm moments away from walking down the aisle. Still, I can't shake this feeling that something's going to go wrong.

And then there's a knock at the door. My heart absolutely thunders that this is it. This is the moment everything goes terribly wrong. At least this time, it won't happen as I'm walking down the aisle. At least this time I can face my heartbreak alone.

My mom opens the door, and Ellie stands there. I can't quite decode the look on her face, but she simply hands my mom an envelope before she leaves.

"For you, Tessi-cat," she says, and I take the envelope from her hands.

Tessa.

The word is written in Tristan's scrawl, and I tear it open.

Tessa,
I knew since I was twelve that this was our destiny.
I'm glad I was right.
I wanted to let you know security is tight. Nobody is getting into our space tonight. No interruptions. Just you, me, Fallon, and the rest of our lives.
I love you.
T and T forever—plus F and L and all the future letters we add to the team.
-Tristan

Tears fill my eyes as I look into the future with this incredible man. Maybe I'm the lucky one, or maybe he is. Maybe we both are.

Or maybe we're just blessed that this is our reality. I think I'll go with that notion.

And then I'm walking down the aisle. The song is even different this time around as I walk down the aisle with Fallon in my arms and my mother beside me. My eyes are on Tristan rather than on the small group of friends who are here in support of us today.

Nobody stops me.

I hand Fallon to my mom just before I get to Tristan, and then he grins at me.

"You made it," he whispers.

"Thank God," I whisper back, and he laughs.

The officiant provided by the hotel says some things about love and commitment, we say our vows, we exchange rings, and then we kiss.

Nobody stops us.

Nobody interrupts us.

Well…not *nobody*. When the officiant asked Tristan if he takes this woman, Fallon let out the sweetest little shriek in her sleep, like she's thrilled and excited her parents are getting married. It drew the sound of laughter from our friends gathered, a lighthearted moment to make this ceremony even more perfect for the two of us.

It's a new beginning. We're done with the heaviness and drama. We may not have control over other people's actions, but we can certainly control our own narrative going forward—a term I learned from my new boss.

We can only control what we do. We can only control our reaction to the outside forces that will surely come along trying to split us apart.

And we will face them together, his hand in mine.

Just as we vowed today: Forever.

Cocktail hour is lovely. The weather is warm as we crest toward the end of July, but the hotel put up a bunch of portable coolers. Maybe it's just because I'm floating on a cloud, but I don't even feel the triple digits. Or maybe I'm a little drunk and that's why I feel like I'm floating. I've had three glasses of champagne after the last nine months of total sobriety.

My mom is keeping Fallon in her room for the night, and Tristan has reserved some suite for the two of us. The sky is dark and we're swaying to some love song when Tristan bends down and whispers in my ear.

"Cocktail hour is over. Time for cock hour."

I giggle. Okay, so he might be a little tipsy himself. I force my features into a pout even though I haven't stopped smiling all night. "Only an hour?"

"Cock hour sounded funnier than cock night."

"What about cock marathon?" I suggest.

"You've got yourself a deal." He draws me in closer so I can feel how hard he is for me against my belly. "Ready to say our goodbyes?" His breath is hot against my ear, and I lean in toward him so my words are just for him.

"Only so I can get you naked."

He raises a brow, presses a soft kiss to my lips, and then we thank our guests, kiss our baby, and take off for the honeymoon suite.

CHAPTER 31

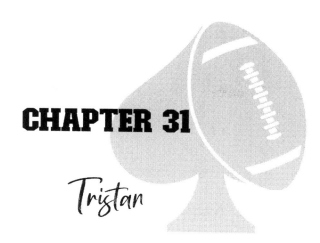

Tristan

You know when you wait for something for more than half your life, and then the day comes, and it's really not what you thought it would be?

I look at the woman in the room with me, and I can't help but think how this moment is what those dreams were made of…but somehow better. More. Perfect.

She is better. More. Perfect.

She's not the teenager I fell in love with. She's a woman now. A wife. A mother. A friend—my *best* friend. A caretaker. She's organized, crafty, smart, and funny. She's real.

She's everything Savannah never was, and I think maybe that was the draw I had to Savannah. I wanted someone who was Tessa's opposite because I hated that we couldn't be together.

Mission accomplished—on both counts, I suppose.

I loosened my tie, and now I take it off and toss it on the dresser.

She's standing near the window, taking off her earrings and setting them on the table beside her. She's sliding the bracelets off her wrists. She's about to reach for the clasp of her necklace, but I want that honor for myself.

I walk over toward her and move in behind her, my front to her back. Her hair is up in some fancy twist, and I lean in toward her, breathing her in as I get close. I unclasp the necklace from behind and set it on the same table with the rest of her jewelry, and then I lean forward and press my lips to her neck.

I inhale as I do it, and it feels like the only breath I'll ever need to take, like I can sustain the rest of my life simply by surviving on her. And in some ways, I suppose that's true. My heart is full, still cracked in some places, but the commitment we made to one another today healed some of those cracks.

We're still missing a member of our family, but we also know he's in good hands. In fact, Miranda called Tessa just yesterday to let us know Logan was released. The rest of his recovery will be at home, and soon school will start again, and though he won't be able to go into the classroom until his immune system is healed, he'll be able to do the same work as his classmates and he'll get to see them via Zoom calls.

I exhale softly before breathing her in again, my lips trailing on her skin.

It's not perfect, but it's damn near as close as we can get. Life is messy and complicated, though, and there's no one else I'd rather straighten it up or simplify it with than the woman I married today.

She tilts her head to the side, giving me better access of her neck, and I offer more kisses. I trail them down her back toward the zipper holding her dress together. I pull it down, the soft zip the only sound in the room aside from the hitch of her breath.

I press kisses to her back as I follow the path, and I unhook the strapless bra she's wearing when I expose the clasp. I pull the dress down her body, and she steps out of it, still facing the windows. I pick the dress up from the floor and set it carefully over a chair, and then I move in behind her again. In the window's reflection, I see her standing before me. She wears only a pair of lacy white panties, and I see her gorgeous, lush tits, her stomach that carried not just one but two babies. All I see is this gorgeous woman who has given me everything I've ever wanted.

I reach around her and feel the soft skin of her stomach.

"It's not how it used to be," she says a little hesitantly.

I spin her around so suddenly that she giggles a little breathlessly until her eyes connect with mine. "Your body is the most beautiful body I have ever seen. You have no idea how sexy you are, do you?"

She shakes her head a little, her eyes darting from mine. "I read that it takes six months or more for most women to return to their pre-pregnancy weight."

My brows dip together as I stare at her. "Look at me."

Her eyes move back to mine. "I still have nine pounds to go."

"You're not listening to me," I scold softly.

She tilts her head a little in confusion.

"I need you to hear me," I say, my voice firm. "You're right. Your body isn't how it used to be." Her face falls a little at my admission until I continue. "*This* body grew our children. It nourished them. It gave them life. I fall more in love with you exactly the way you are every single day, and you better not for a second doubt that." I get down onto my knees and kiss her stomach, and then I move up to kiss her breasts, thumbing one nipple while I suck another into my mouth. "God, I love the way you feel," I murmur, and then I sink back down to my knees and shove my face right between her legs, inhaling deeply. "And the way you smell." My tongue moves to her clit, where I suck for a beat as her legs start to tremble. "And the way you taste." I stand and look down into her eyes. "I love every single thing about you, Tessa Higgins."

"God, I love you," she says, and I lower my lips to hers so she can taste her tang in my mouth. I feel her heart pounding against mine, but there are clothes separating us—my shirt and tie, my pants. Underwear.

I devour her with my kiss, but it slows as she pulls back. She smiles up at me sweetly even though she's got me panting, and then she slowly unbuttons my shirt. One by one, she slides the button through the hole. Down, down, down with the sort of aching slowness that only builds the anticipation between us.

Once it's fully open, she pulls the fabric open and slides it down my arms until it lands on the floor behind me. Her hands immediately find purchase on my chest. She slides her palms across my skin and down to my abdomen, her fingertips tracing the ridges of the muscles there—more pronounced than they used to be after the weeks of heavy workouts after she went back to Iowa and I stayed in Vegas.

She tugs at the waistband of my pants then snags her bottom lip between her teeth as she unbuckles my belt. My cock is painfully hard, and my entire body aches for her. I've always wanted her. Sex has always been amazing with her. We've always had an intense emotional connection.

But tonight, this is something else entirely. It has more meaning. More feeling. More everything. It's the first night of forever.

She finally slides the zipper down and pulls my cock out. It's hard and heavy in her hands, and she slides her other hand down further to cup my balls.

I groan my satisfaction, and she handles them gently. Her hands are perfect on me as she tugs at my cock the way she knows I like it, but tonight, the primal urge to be inside her intoxicates me. I halt her progress by backing up, and then I grab her up into my arms. She reacts with a squeal, and I toss her onto the bed. I pull my pants and boxers off, leaving them in a pile on the floor, and I stalk toward her.

I rip her panties down her legs in one swoop, and then I dive back into her pussy face-first. I lick my way through her slick folds, the taste of her only serving to make every bone in my body ache to be inside her.

It's too much and not enough at the same time.

She grips onto the bedding as I stop to suck on her swollen clit, her hips jutting up to meet my mouth with every lash of my tongue against her.

I finally stop but only because the ache is unbearable. I move up the bed to hover over her, and then I line my cock up with her pussy and thrust my way home.

She lets go of her grip on the sheets only to clutch onto me. Her nails dig into my back as I pump into her, my lips finding hers and not letting go. She lets out a soft cry of pleasure when I slow down, my only goal to make this version of paradise last a little longer.

"Oh God, Tristan," she moans, and then her pussy clenches over me. "I'm coming," she says over and over as her pussy contracts and her entire body shudders with her release. Her soft moans paired with the way her body's moving beneath mine send me into my own orgasm. I pull out as the masculine need to mark her as mine fills me, and I grab my cock in my hand, jerking it until I spill all over her stomach. When my swollen dick starts to calm, I gently roll the head of it through the come I left behind.

There's something insanely hot about seeing my come all over her. She belongs to me. She always did, but today we made that commitment, and now forever can begin.

CHAPTER 32

Tessa

He gently wipes my stomach clean, and then he lies beside me and whispers to me about what a perfect day this has been and what a perfect life we will have, and the way he takes care of me feels so romantic even after he jerked off all over my stomach.

God, that was hot.

He is hot. He's way out of my league, and yet somehow, he chose me. There are times when the doubt creeps in and tells me he's only with me because he wants to save me, he's only with me because of our shared history—or whatever other justification I can try to rationalize in my brain.

But the truth of the matter is that he chose me because there's this mutual understanding between the two of us that connects us down to our very souls, and that's something nobody else would ever be able to measure up to.

My mom decided to stay in Vegas for the next week, and we stay at the hotel in the honeymoon suite for a few extra nights. We keep Fallon with us for the most part, touring Vegas as he introduces me to my new home during the day and making love to me into the wee hours of the night. My mom takes Fallon for a few hours at a time or sometimes overnight so we can have a little time off to spend as newlyweds, but we only have five official days before he has to leave for training camp.

And those five blissful days pass in the blink of an eye.

He's gearing up for training camp in between helping me get to know our new town, and in those hours Ellie is training me and getting me up to speed with all things Prince Charming Public Relations. She has an assistant, Leah, who is another football wife. She's sweet and has already befriended me, and both of them took me to the Complex one morning to introduce me to everyone I need to know.

Mama Mo, the Coach's wife, is my favorite.

It feels like I have another mom here in Vegas to look after me, and I'm already seeing how much of a family the Vegas Aces really are.

Elizabeth has been amazing with the addition of Fallon to the daily play group she nannies for, and she called me in once when Nolan tripped and skinned his knee to employ my pediatric nursing skills once again.

I loved helping him feel better. I loved wiping away his tears after I put a bandage over his boo boo. I loved being helpful in this place where everyone has been so wonderfully welcoming.

Before I know it, we're saying goodbye to my mom at the airport as she heads back to Iowa—his parents left a few days ago—and spending Wednesday night back at Luke and Ellie's house. It's our last night before training camp begins, the event that kicks off the season for players.

He just gave me my second orgasm of the night, and I'm grateful once again for the privacy separating our room from the sitting room where Fallon sleeps peacefully.

We lie together breathlessly, neither of us moving as we both feel like jello after that intense round.

"Does that get better every time?" he asks, voicing the thoughts in my head.

"I think somehow it does," I murmur, and he chuckles.

"You sound sleepy."

I sigh as I stare up at the ceiling. "I guess I just...don't want this moment to end."

"I don't either," he murmurs. He turns in toward me, but I keep my gaze up at the ceiling as I think about how the next two weeks are going to be so strange without him. And the next six months, really. He'll be around after the first two weeks in California, but his mind will be on the game.

I've never been with him in season, and now we're married. It's one adventure after another, that's for sure.

"I know I need to get up to pee, but I also don't ever want to move. And I don't want you to leave tomorrow." A tear slides from the side of my eye down into my hairline.

Tristan's fingertips come up to brush the tear away. "It's only two weeks, and we'll talk every day," he promises.

"I know we will." I want to say more. I want to tell him that it's harder for the person staying behind. He gets to go off on his football adventure and I'll be here learning a new city and learning more about my new job and boss and taking care of a newborn all on my own.

It feels like a tremendously overwhelming amount of weight to carry, but I knew what I was getting into with him, and instead of saying any of that, I choose to focus on all the positive in our lives.

After seven long years apart, seven years of heartbreak and darkness, the sun is shining once again. There are rainbows of hope in an endless sky.

"Fallon's going to miss her daddy," I whisper.

"I'm going to miss her, too. Both my girls," he says, and he presses a kiss to my temple. I finally turn to mirror him, and our eyes connect. The heat passes through our locked gaze like always, but the tenderness and pure love there are dominant. "But we've got this. Two weeks, and then I'll be back, and I'll be whining about how my hamstring is sore and you can put those nursing skills to work and help me get game-ready again."

I chuckle. "I'll be waiting." Anything to get my hands on those sexy hamstrings of his.

We've been through a lot, but we've made our way to the other side. Now is when we begin our forever. This is where we settle into married life, where we really put the past behind us along with the secrets and the lies and the manipulators.

This is where our happily ever after begins.

CHAPTER 33

Tristan

Time flies when you're having fun, right?

And somehow, time has flown by at a breakneck pace.

It slowed significantly once I arrived in California to spend time at the vineyard where the Aces hold our first two weeks of training camp. The two weeks were grueling both physically and mentally. It's hard fighting my best friends for my place on the field. If I'm starting, that means Travis probably isn't. Josh Nolan and I were the predetermined starters, but the first two weeks of camp have allowed us to keep those jobs intact.

But I'm a little worse for the wear because of it.

I'm thankful for the intensity I put into my pre-camp workouts. Some guys are in a lot worse shape than me, but I'm still sore. I'm still exhausted. I still know we have more weeks of camp and exhibition games before the season officially kicks off and the real fun begins.

We have one day off to heal before the intensity starts up again, and I plan to spend every second I can with my new wife. We didn't have nearly enough time celebrating our union before I had to leave, and now that I'm back, I have big plans to make up for it.

As the plane touches down back in Vegas, I feel that sense of home again.

Our physical home might not be ready quite yet, but wherever Tessa is…that's home. And it always will be.

She's adapted well to Vegas, and she fits right in with the group who has welcomed us into not just their home, but their lives. And when I burst through the front door, she stands there waiting with our baby in her arms and a smile on her face.

"Welcome home, husband," she says softly, and I press a soft kiss to her lips, to the baby's forehead, and then a longer one to Tessa's mouth.

I lean my forehead down to hers. "God, I missed you, wife," I murmur.

"I missed you, too," she says. She hands me Fallon, who's awake. She looks different already. She's a little over two months old, and in the last two weeks, she's grown. Her little cheeks are fuller, she seems longer, and I already feel like I've missed so much.

But I'm back now. I still have the long hours of training camp here at home in front of me, but at least I get to come home to my girls at the end of the day.

"How's the hamstring?" she asks.

"So far, so good," I say. "But I will always take a massage from my favorite nurse."

"I'll give you more than a hamstring massage," she says, and she winks.

I laugh. That's my girl, and that gives me an idea. "Hey, I have tomorrow off…you want to go out tonight?"

She narrows her eyes at me. "Where?"

"I could take you to a nightclub, or we could go dancing, or…" I lower my voice and whisper close to her ear since we're in the Daltons' foyer. "I could have you sign an NDA and take you as a guest to Coax."

Her brows draw together, and then a look of total curiosity flashes in her eyes. "The NDA," she demands.

I laugh. I guess I'm taking my girl to Coax. "Get ready for a very interesting evening."

She squirms a little. "After two weeks away from you, I think we might need to get one of the private rooms for ourselves."

I raise a brow. "Deal." And then I text Heidi and ask her to put me on the list for a private room for tonight...for at least a two-hour block.

I'm nervous to take her there. I haven't been back there myself in months—not since Tessa and I got together, and I feel like this will be a completely different experience than the other times I've gone.

I don't bother asking Travis, Jaxon, or Cory if they'll be there. Maybe they will, maybe they won't, but tonight is about reconnecting with my *wife* after way too long apart.

"Tristan is taking me out tonight. Any chance you can watch Fallon?" I hear Tessa ask Ellie as I walk up the stairs with my duffel bag.

"Of course. You two kids have fun," Ellie says.

I chuckle. If only she knew where we were going.

Maybe we should tell her. She and Luke seem like the type who would enjoy a night of fun there, but some secrets are better kept...well, secret. Especially from my publicist, who would surely try to talk me out of going there, let alone being an actual paid member.

I drive, and when I pull up out front and put the car in park, I glance over at her.

Her brows are knit together in confusion. "This...isn't what I was expecting."

"What were you expecting?"

She lifts a shoulder. "I don't know. But this just looks like a house. A mansion, really, but still. Not a...*sex club*."

I chuckle. "It's more than a sex club. Yes, that takes place here, but it's a safe place for people with means to hang out. No paparazzi. No cell phones. Fewer worries than your average nightclub, you know?"

She nods, and I walk around to help her out of the car. She chose a tight black dress that shows off her delicious curves in the most mouthwatering way, and I can't wait to peel it off her, toss it on the floor, and satisfy the need that has been coursing through me for two long weeks.

We greet Rodney at the doorway, and he sends us in with a friendly greeting. Heidi's at the reception desk as usual, and she takes our phones along with Tessa's signed NDA. She informs us that Troy is our host tonight.

Tessa glances at me as if to ask *Troy who?* She probably has about a million other questions just like I did the first time I came here, and I'm ready to show her what this place is all about.

With that in mind, I open the door and lead my wife into the club.

CHAPTER 34

Tessa

When I first learned that my husband was a member of a sex club, I pictured people having sex in every room. Maybe even out in front of the place.

To my surprise, that's not at all what this is.

It's a mansion built into the foothills of some mountain. It stands by itself in the desert, and it's both elegant and imposing. Except for the house lights and landscape lighting that's almost romantic, it's also dark, as if every window has heavy curtains on it. If not for the cars parked out front, I would have no idea that anybody's even here.

The reception desk is elegant. The woman sitting behind it is elegant.

As Tristan leads me into the first room…more elegance.

To my disappointment, nobody's even naked.

And then I realize it's because it's really *not* a sex club. It's an exclusive club for exclusive people. The first room which looks to take up half the first floor is basically a standard nightclub. Music pumps, and people dance while they drink. They all seem to be having a nice time, and they're completely oblivious to the fact that a football megastar just walked into the room.

Or maybe they're not *totally* oblivious, but they don't really seem to care.

We walk through the nightclub toward the other half of the first floor, which is set up sort of like a study. I can't hear the music from the room next to us except when someone enters the room, and even then, it's somehow muted.

Bookcases line the walls, and there are several seating areas of different sizes. Two wingback armchairs sit with a small table in between, and there are four sets of those along one side of the room. A couch and two love seats all face a table for bigger groups to talk, and there are three sets of those. Pool tables are lined up in the middle of the room with pendant lighting overhead, and a long bar with stools extends along another wall.

This looks like a room where business is conducted, and I glance around the room. My eyes land on legendary baseball player Troy Bodine talking with a group of other baseball players I recognize.

"Troy Bodine?" I murmur to Tristan, who nods.

"One of the owners," he says.

My eyes land on the hottest former baseball player in the group: Cooper Noah.

He played for the Dodgers for many years and quit playing thanks to an elbow injury not too long ago. I recognize him from some magazine's cover—he made the *hottest celebrity* list for the last six years running, and even from across the room, he's hotter than that magazine gave him credit for. He rakes a hand through his perfectly mussed dark hair then runs his hand along the strong jawline. He glances up, probably because he feels me staring at him, and he offers a friendly smile.

Jeez.

His teeth practically gleam even in the darkness of this room, and I swear his bright blue eyes sparkle at me.

Tristan chooses that moment to toss his arm around my shoulder and draw me in.

"That's Cooper Noah," I whisper yell, and he chuckles.

"I know. I've met him a few times. Super nice guy."

"What's he doing here?" I ask.

He shrugs. "Looks like he's talking to Troy." And then he starts walking over toward the bar like it's no big deal that Cooper Noah and Troy Bodine are just sitting on a couch in a club. "Want a drink?"

I nod. "A glass of wine would really hit the spot." Or two or three.

It's weird to look around the room and spot more people I recognize. Do these people use the sex rooms?

And speaking of the sex rooms…when are we going to see them? Do I get to watch Cooper in a sex room?

Tristan orders, and I'm standing beside him as we wait for the bartender when I hear male voices behind me.

"Thanks for inviting me to the club tonight, man," the first voice says. "This floor is great, but the third floor isn't really my thing."

I'm so freaking tempted to turn around to see who it is.

"I had ulterior motives," the second voice says.

"You always do," the first voice says with an easy laugh, and without knowing anything about them, I can tell it's two friends talking.

"I'm sure you've heard by now the expansion team was approved. Las Vegas is getting a new baseball team, and they've given me an offer to be the manager. I want you to come play for me," voice two says.

I can't help it.

I turn to look behind me, and my eyes widen as I pretend I'm looking at something across the room. Both men glance at me, totally catching me in the act of trying to see who they are.

My cheeks flush with embarrassment as I turn back around.

Oh. My. God.

It's Troy Bodine and Cooper Noah.

Good Lord, they're both attractive men.

This isn't a sex club.

This is a club where the hottest people on Earth get to gather and just sit around being hot.

Troy is asking Cooper to play for the expansion team coming to Vegas, and I've never felt so on the cutting edge of the hottest celebrity gossip in my entire twenty-five years on this Earth.

"Nah, man. I've been out of the game for years. You don't want me," Cooper says as I pretend to watch the bartender when my attention is solely focused on the conversation happening behind me.

"Is the elbow healed?" Troy asks.

"Yeah. Surgery pieced me back together, but I'm far from being in shape to play," Cooper says.

Troy huffs out a laugh. "Then it's a good thing we've got five months of off-season training before we need to head into pre-season training."

"You really want me to unretire?" Cooper asks. "I don't know. I mean, I miss the game, of course. I loved every second of playing. But I've got some good shit going on now, too."

Troy's not laughing anymore. "Listen, Coop. You know how these expansion drafts go. Everyone holds tight to their best players, and we get our pick from the leftovers. We need you. We need a born leader. We need someone to be the face of the Vegas Kings, and I want that someone to be you."

"The Vegas Kings?" Cooper asks, and I wish I could see Troy behind me. I make a guess that he nods at Cooper's question. "That's a kickass name."

It really is.

Tristan hands me a glass of wine and grabs his beer, and then he turns around. "Hey, man," he says to Cooper, and he nods at Troy.

He *knows* them.

He's *friends* with them.

My mind is blown.

He ushers me up to the next floor, so I never get to hear Cooper's response.

He takes me through the strip club and out to the backyard, a romantic area with a pool and a gorgeous view of the mountain right in front of us.

We head up to the third floor, and rather than take me on a tour, Tristan opens a door. He holds it open and gestures with his hand, so I walk in first. It's dark, and he flips a switch behind me as he locks the door.

Lights turn on, but they're dim. That's when I notice the dimmer, but Tristan leaves it how it is.

The room is large, with a dresser on one side, a leather chair in one corner, and a huge bed on a rotating platform in the center with a nightstand beside it.

Is there a bed size bigger than a king? Because I'm pretty sure this room has it.

Built into the headboard and footboard are what look to be cuffs, and a little thrill goes through me at the thought of being stretched, cuffed, and pleasured.

Mirrors of different sizes and shapes are on the walls, and there's even a mirror on the ceiling.

It seems no matter which way I look, I'll be able to watch whatever Tristan is doing to me.

"This is one of the private rooms," Tristan says, moving in behind me. "Nobody can see what we're doing in here." He points to the corners of the rooms. "No cameras. Total privacy."

I set my wine glass down on the dresser. "What plans do you have for me, Mr. Higgins?"

I open the top dresser drawer, and my eyes widen at what I find.

Vibrators, dildos, and cock rings of all different sizes stare back at me.

I quickly slam the drawer shut as I spin around to face my husband, who stealthily moved mere inches from me.

I gasp at his proximity.

"Find something you like in there, Mrs. Higgins?" he murmurs.

"Uh…" I stammer.

"Everything in here is sanitized and ready for use." He pulls open the next drawer, showing me a variety of crops, whips, and paddles. The next drawer has clamps and plugs and other items that seem to be a total mystery to my rather naïve, innocent self.

I glance up at him. "Or we could just…you know…"

"Fuck?" he asks, and the way he says the word with a hard *k* sound at the end speaks right to my aching vagina.

I nod a little timidly, and he shuts the drawer and steps toward me. I shiver—not because I'm cold, but because of the anticipation. Because I can't believe he's really here in front of me.

Yeah, it was exciting seeing those other athletes and celebrities downstairs. It was neat hearing that Las Vegas is getting a baseball team, and Troy Bodine wants Cooper Noah to be the face of it.

But it's all gone from my mind as I focus on Tristan.

My *husband*.

The man who has vowed forever with me when for the last seven years, the only way I had a chance to even get in touch with him was in my dreams.

I draw in a deep breath and exhale slowly as he wraps his arms around me, I breathe him in, and I tip my chin up so I can look at him. So I can pinch myself. So I can remind myself that this is real.

And then his mouth collides down to mine, and he devours me with a simple kiss. My heart races and I hold him tightly, pulling myself as close to him as I can while he kisses me with all the pent-up passion of being away from each other for two long weeks.

His hand glides along my torso to my breast, which he cups in his big hand, and then he backs up a little, stopping the kiss way too abruptly.

"Take off your dress," he demands, and I practically squeal with excitement as I scramble out of my dress.

I *love* demanding, dominating, aggressive Tristan.

I also love sweet cinnamon roll Tristan who's sexy on the outside and sweet on the inside. And caretaker Tristan who does everything he can to be a wholesome, good guy. And hot as hell football player in the tight pants Tristan. And best daddy in the world Tristan who's a family man down to his very core.

And by some miracle, he loves me, too.

Which he shows me quite aggressively as my hands and feet are cuffed to this bed. First he sucks on my clit, giving me an intense orgasm with his mouth that has me trembling, and then he slides into me and gives me another one.

I'm sated, exhausted, and elated as we rest on the bed together for a little while before he's ready to go again, and it's in those quiet moments of bliss that I look toward the future. I see laughter and intimacy and more kids and quiet getaways and loud vacations. I see so much happiness and bliss when I spent so many years in the opposite.

It always came back to that one person—the one who was meant for me just as I am meant for him.

And I can't wait for every second of the future with my wide receiver.

EPILOGUE

Tristan

three months later

Jack Dalton throws the ball as I lunge to get open. I know where to go, but I can already tell this guy's mission is to stay right on my ass all day.

I'm faster than him, though. The ball falls right into my hands, and I take off running like the fucking wind.

My hamstring feels good today as we face the Seahawks. I score the first points of the game as I cross into the end zone, and I fist bump the camera to say hi to my son just like I promised. Logan is doing amazingly well, and he's even been cleared to attend school in-person. He's excelling in science, and I can't wait to see what the future holds for him.

I point up at the sky next, just like I promised Tessa I would since she's my whole world. I find her in the stands, and I hold my hand to my heart next as I grin. That's for Fallon, who holds my heart in her sweet little hands.

It's the same every time I score. Fist bump, point at the sky, search for my girls and cover my heart. And then I wave, too. That's for my mom and dad.

I run to the sidelines, where my teammates slap my ass or knock into my helmet. Coach Jeff shows me how I could've run a slightly different route to get open more easily, but I'm only half-listening as I celebrate the points I just put up.

I sit on the bench and some kid hands me a cup. I drain it as Travis sits on the bench beside me, both of us breathing heavily after the run we just made.

"Nice play, man. Did Jeff already tell you how you could've run to the left instead?"

I laugh. "Of course he did."

Coach wanted to experiment with something new this season—something that worked well in the first few games of the season. Because Jack Dalton has a perfect arm and his preference is to throw the ball, we're switching back and forth between a three and four wide receiver set offense. It exhausts the opposing defense since they're always chasing after us, giving us the chance at more points. And that means more playing time for Travis this season since he's one of our top receivers.

Our offense is incredible, and our defense is working hard.

I feel it already. It feels like we're heading toward the big game.

I feel so... *free* this season.

Last year, I was weighed down by being with the wrong woman. I was hurting after I saw Tessa with another man at her father's funeral.

But this year, everything has fallen into place.

We're moving into our new house tomorrow. We'll finally be in our own space to live as a family. As much as I've loved living with Luke and Ellie, I'm ready.

I'm ready to fuck my wife in our huge new bedroom without worrying that someone down the hall can hear us.

I'm ready to walk naked through my kitchen whenever I damn well please.

I'm ready to take my wife on the kitchen island, or in the pool, or on the staircase.

I still can't believe everything that happened in the off-season. Between finding Tessa and almost losing her again, getting divorced, attempting to get married, having a baby, meeting my son, donating bone marrow, and actually getting married, I have to admit...I'm grateful to be back in season.

It was one adventure after another, but I thrive on routine.

And I love this routine.

I practice hard Wednesday through Saturday, play on Sunday, and, if we win, I have Monday and Tuesday off. Except for our eight away games this season, I'm home a good amount of time. I get to watch my girl as she grows, and I get to spend time with my new wife. It's true that in some ways, I'm married to the game, but in other ways, I still get to be a family man. It's all about balance, and I feel like I've finally found it.

I score once more during the game, and after I shower, change, and talk to the press, I walk out into the family area next to the locker rooms. I find Tessa standing there with my parents. My dad is looking great and my mom is holding Fallon. I kiss Tessa first, Fallon second, and my mother third as my dad pats my shoulder.

"Great game, kiddo," he says.

Travis sidles up beside me, and my mom hands him a bag of puppy chow. I laugh at their little inside joke as he hugs both my parents. In a lot of ways, he's the brother I never had. I'm glad to see him get more playing time this season, and every week at our wide receivers' dinner, I tell him he's next.

And he tells me how whipped I am.

He assures me he'll never be that way.

I assure him he will...when the right woman comes along.

And then he gets a sad, faraway look in his eyes. I can tell he's not convinced the right woman will *ever* come along. He always quickly changes the subject, but I can tell something's on his mind.

I'll get it out of him soon enough.

"Don't worry," my mom says to me, bumping my shoulder with hers. "I made some for you, too." She glances over at Tessa. "And I made you your own bag this time so your husband can't steal it."

We all get a good laugh, and then they head back to their hotel while we head to Luke's to pack up the last of our things before the big move tomorrow.

And then moving day is upon us. Fallon coos happily in her carrier while we sign the paperwork, and then we grab our keys and head over to our new home.

We've been here practically every day over the last couple months, watching as each final touch was put into place. All the furniture is set to be delivered later today, and my parents will be spending the night in their casita. Janet is coming next week to visit and to check out her new digs.

Somehow every dream I ever had has become my reality.

I have the greatest job in the world playing professional football for the greatest team in the league with best friends who have become family to me. I'm married to the only woman I've ever loved, and we share not one but two incredible children. We're already talking about expanding our family.

With a dog, first.

But eventually, with more children. I want to fill this giant house with chaos and laughter to really complete the dream, and I know it's just down the road.

Favorite MISTAKE

We might've made a lot of mistakes to get here, but of all the mistakes that added up to where we are right now…this one's my favorite.

THE END

ACKNOWLEDGMENTS

Thank you first as always to Matt. I love being on this ride with you and our two little cuties.

Thank you to Autumn Gantz of Wordsmith Publicity for being my sounding board, my first reader, my proofreader, and my right hand.

Thank you to Trenda London for the content editing and your hand in making this series everything it was meant to be.

Thank you to Diane Holtry for being my amazing longtime beta reader. I value your insight and your friendship.

Thank you to my ARC Team, members of the Vegas Aces Spoiler Room and Team LS, and all the bloggers and influencers for reading, reviewing, posting, and sharing.

And finally, thank YOU! Thanks for reading the Vegas Aces. I'm not leaving this world anytime soon, although we're taking a baseball detour this spring since Cooper Noah is very excited to share his story starting with *Curveball*. I'll be back later in the year with Travis Woods and his *Fumbled* pass…

Cheers until we meet again next season!

xoxo,
Lisa Suzanne

ABOUT THE AUTHOR

Lisa Suzanne is a romance author who resides in Arizona with her husband and two kids. She's a former high school English teacher and college composition instructor. When she's not cuddling or chasing her kids, she can be found working on her latest book or watching reruns of *Friends*.

ALSO BY LISA SUZANNE

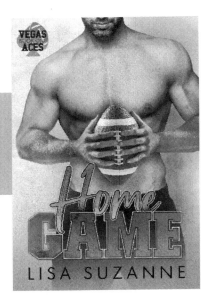

HOME GAME
Vegas Aces Book One
#1 Bestselling Sports Romance

A LITTLE LIKE DESTINY
A Little Like Destiny Book One
#1 Bestselling Rock Star Romance

Printed in Great Britain
by Amazon